Bhawna

Best of
Akbar Birbal
TALES

TINY TOT PUBLICATIONS
INDIA

Best of
Akbar Birbal
TALES

© TINY TOT PUBLICATIONS 2006
This Edition:-2008

Retold & Edited by:

Shyam Dua

Published By:

TINY TOT PUBLICATIONS

235, Jagriti Enclave,
Vikas Marg,
Delhi-110092 (INDIA)
Ph.: 2216 7314, 2216 3582,
Fax:- 91-11-22143023
email: tinytotpub@hotmail.com

ISBN : 81-304-0333-1

Illustrated by
Rustagi. P. R.

CONTENTS

THE COST OF THE EMPEROR

Emperor Akbar was very impressed by the intelligence of Birbal. Whenever he felt bored of royal works, he talked to him. One day, after completing his work, Akbar was sitting with his courtiers and was joking with them. The topic was the costly things of the world. Just then, the Emperor asked, "Birbal, tell me my price."

All the courtiers felt happy to hear the question. They thought that Birbal would not be able to answer the question and would be humiliated in the court. But Birbal was very clever. He said, "Lord, to quote the price of something is the work of jewellers. If you permit, I will ask all the jewellers of the city to come to the court tomorrow. They can give the correct answer of your question."

The emperor had asked the question in amusement. He readily permitted Birbal. On Birbal's command, all the jewellers came to the court the next day. They saluted the king and

asked, "O King, what can we do for you?"

The emperor signalled Birbal. Birbal said, "You have to tell the price of the emperor."

On hearing Birbal, all the jewellers stared at one another. They had thought that the emperor would ask them to make jewellery for his queens. But they were facing a big problem.

The head of the jewellers mustered some courage and said, "Lord, we are not prepared to answer this question. Please give us some time. We will discuss this matter and, then, tell you the answer."

The emperor permitted them. He also sent Birbal with them. He knew that those jewellers would not be able to find the answer on their own. On the other hand, Birbal had already thought of the answer. The jewellers discussed the matter. After much time, when they could not come out with an answer, they looked at Birbal with hope. Birbal knew that this would happen. He told his plan to the leader. Then, he asked him to go to the emperor with all the jewellers again and ask for fifteen days time to answer the question.

The jewellers went to the court and said to the emperor, "Lord, we could not come up with the

answer. We request you to give us fifteen days." The emperor agreed. On the other side, Birbal went to the mint and ordered for a slightly bigger coin than normal coins. The coin was ready the next day. Birbal sent the coin to the leader of the jewellers.

On the sixteenth day, all the jewellers reached the court. Birbal was already present there. The leader took out the big coin from a bag and gave it to the emperor. He said, "O Lord, this is your price."

"My price is just one coin!" exclaimed the emperor.

The leader said with folded hands, "Lord, this is not an ordinary coin. It is the biggest coin and is rare. Likewise, you are rare and one of your kind."

The emperor smiled at the words of the leader. He looked at Birbal. He knew Birbal had helped the jewellers. He gifted many presents to the jewellers.

THE UNWANTED GUEST

The cleverness of Birbal was not only famous in India, but also in other countries. One day, the Emperor of Turkistan decided to test the cleverness of Birbal. He sent his clever minister with a letter to Agra. After travelling for many days, the minister reached the court of Emperor Akbar. He introduced himself and gave Akbar the letter. The letter read, "Salute to the Emperor of India. My minister wants to see the magnificent city of Agra. Please allow him to live there for as many days as he wants."

Emperor Akbar could say nothing to the unwanted guest. He consulted Birbal on how to send the guest back to his country. Birbal asked some soldiers to make arrangements for the minister to stay in the weakest fort of Agra. When the minister went out of the court, Birbal said to the emperor, "Let's see for how long he has planned to stay here. If he leaves within a few days, its okay otherwise, I have a plan."

The minister started living there lavishly. He had all the comforts of life. Many days passed by but the minister showed no sign of leaving.

Akbar called Birbal and told him the problem. Birbal asked him not to worry. He asked some soldiers to break the ramparts of the fort at night in which the minister was staying. He also asked some mahouts to make their elephants run amok around the fort. All was done according to the plan. People were not aware of anything. They thought an earthquake had arrived. They started running helter-skelter.

Next morning, the minister went to the court and said to the emperor, "Sir, from where were those noises coming last night? I am very scared."

At this, Birbal said, "Sir, actually an earthquake hit the city last night. Here, it is very frequent. God save us all. We are also very scared."

The minister thought, 'I should better run away from here or else I will die.'

He sought the emperor's permission to leave for his country. Akbar felt very happy and at once permitted the minister. He also gave many gifts for the Emperor of Turkistan.

After travelling for many days, the minister reached his city. He told whatever had happened at Agra to his

emperor. The emperor understood that Birbal had befooled his intelligent minister. The minister also realised his foolishness. He praised the clever Birbal within his heart.

On the other side, Emperor Akbar thanked Birbal for helping him. Birbal smiled and said, "It is okay. I am always at your service."

Emperor Akbar embraced clever Birbal and gave him many gifts.

THE RIDDLE

Emperor Akbar was once wandering in the royal garden in a joyous mood. Just then, Birbal reached there. Akbar asked him a riddle–

"There are two lids. In between, there are many watermelons. What is the thing that gets finished on its own just like wax melts down on getting heated?"

Birbal thought for some time but could not think of an answer. He said to the emperor, "Please give me some time. I will definitely give you the answer to this riddle." The emperor gave him the time.

Birbal knew a farmer who was an expert in solving riddles. He lived on the outskirts of the city in a village. Birbal went to the house of the farmer, but he was not there. His daughter was cooking food.

Birbal asked the girl, " What are you doing?"

"I am burning the mother and cooking the daughter," replied the girl.

Birbal then asked her, "Where is your father?"

"He has gone to mix soil in soil," said the girl.

"And your mother?" asked Birbal again.

"She has gone to convert one-one into two-two," replied the girl with a smile on her face.

Birbal couldn't understand any of the replies of the girl. But he thought that if the daughter was clever, her father would be cleverer. After a while, the father entered the cottage. When he saw Birbal in his cottage, he welcomed him and gave him a good hospitality. Then, Birbal asked him about the replies of her daughter. The farmer said, "At the first question, the girl said that she was burning the mother and cooking the daughter. She meant that she was cooking *arhar dal* on the flames of *arhar* wood. The answer to the second question was that I had gone to mix soil with soil. Actually I had gone to the cemetery to attend the last rituals of my friend. The third answer was that the mother had gone to convert one-one into two-two. That means the mother had gone to collect wheat."

On listening the meaning of the three answers, Birbal got stunned. He stared at the little girl. He thought that such a girl was very rare of her kind.

Birbal said to the farmer, "I have come to ask you for help. Will you solve one riddle for me?"

"Yes, sure. What is the riddle," said the farmer. Birbal told him the riddle which the emperor had asked him to solve.

On hearing the riddle, the farmer said, "This riddle is very easy. The two lids are the earth and the heaven. The watermelons are the people on this earth. Just as wax melts down on being heated, human beings die when their time comes." Birbal thanked the farmer for helping him. He went to the emperor and told him the answer. The emperor felt happy and gave presents to Birbal.

TWO HANDFUL OF COLD

It was very cold in Delhi. People were shivering with cold. They would wear woollen clothes at the time of going out.

One evening, Emperor Akbar and Birbal were roaming in the city in disguise. Suddenly, the Emperor asked Birbal, "How cold is it today?"

Birbal was surprised. At that time, no device had been invented to measure temperature. Birbal thought what answer to give to the emperor.

Suddenly, Birbal's eyes fell on an old man who was sitting on the roadside. He was sitting with clinched fists because of extreme cold. He quickly said, "Lord, it is two handful of cold."

On hearing the answer, the emperor was surprised. He asked, "How can you say that?"

Birbal pointed at the old man who was sitting with his two fists clinched. The emperor stared at Birbal and smiled at him.

THE WEIGHT OF THE GOAT

Emperor Akbar used to feel pleasure on putting challenges in front of Birbal. Birbal also loved to give strange answers to Emperor Akbar.

One day, Emperor Akbar gave a goat to Birbal and said, "Birbal, keep this goat with you for one month. She should be given food at proper time. I will check her weight after one month. Keep in mind that its weight should not decrease or increase during this period."

Birbal understood that the emperor had again made a plan to test his intelligence. He thought of a plan. He took the goat to his house. For one month, the goat lived at Birbal's house. During this period, Birbal took good care of the goat.

After one month, when Birbal reached the court, Emperor Akbar asked him, "How is the goat?"

"She is absolutely fine," said Birbal. "I hope she didn't lose her weight," asked Akbar.

"No," said Birbal. "Weigh her and see for yourself."

On hearing this, the emperor was surprised. He was not expecting such an answer. "I think you didn't give her enough to eat," said the emperor.

"But I always fed her to her fill," said Birbal.

Akbar knew that Birbal was not lying. He had appointed several spies to keep an eye on him. He ordered his men to weigh the goat. The goat's weight was same as earlier. "How did you do this, Birbal?" asked Akbar.

"O Lord, I used to feed her whole day long, and at night I used to make her stand in front of the cage of a lion. She used to get scared and lose all her weight. In this way I maintained her weight," said Birbal. Everybody in the court praised Birbal for his intelligence.

TO CRY OR TO LAUGH

One day some guests arrived at the Mughal court. On the moonlit night, all the guests were invited for the dinner with the emperor. At the scheduled time, the guests reached the palace. Birbal was already present there to welcome the guests. He embraced all the guests one by one. After an introduction with one another, one guest asked Birbal, "What happened? The emperor has still not arrived?"

At this, Birbal said, "He is just coming. May be he got stuck in some important work."

All the guests waited for the emperor for a long time. Just then, an attendant came running and said to Birbal, "Sir, the emperor's aunt has died."

All the guests offered their condolences. After some time, again an attendant came running and

informed, "The elder queen has given birth to a boy."

After some time, it was announced, "The emperor is coming." Now the guests were in a fix. They could not understand whether they should offer condolences to the emperor on his aunt's death or congratulate him on his son's birth. They asked Birbal to solve their problem. Birbal said, "First see the mood of the emperor. If he seems happy, congratulate him, but if he seems sad, offer him your condolences." All the guests thanked Birbal for solving their problem.

THE MONTH OF RAMZAN

One day, Emperor Akbar was sitting in the court and talking with his courtiers. Just then, he asked everyone, "Does Ramzan come and go happily or sadly?"

All the courtiers were surprised to hear such a strange question. Then one of them said, "Lord, Ramzan always comes happily."

At this, Emperor Akbar said, "How can you say that? Can anyone take the guarantee of this answer?"

Everyone in the court stared at each other and kept mum. When the emperor could not get answer from anyone, he looked at Birbal with hope. "Birbal, can you give the answer of the question?"

"Lord, the month of Ramzan comes with happiness," replied Birbal.

"How can you say so?" asked the emperor. "Lord, the month of Ramzan goes every year and comes back the next year. Had it gone back with sadness, it would have never returned." The emperor got satisfied with the answer and praised Birbal.

THE THREE QUALITIES

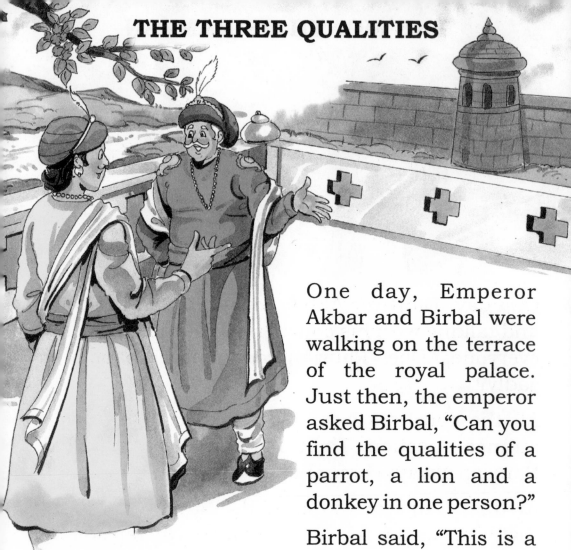

One day, Emperor Akbar and Birbal were walking on the terrace of the royal palace. Just then, the emperor asked Birbal, "Can you find the qualities of a parrot, a lion and a donkey in one person?"

Birbal said, "This is a very simple task. I will present such a man in the court tomorrow."

Next day, a man reached the palace on a palanquin. He went to the court and saluted the emperor. Then, Birbal asked an attendant to bring a jar of wine and glass. The attendant soon returned with the two things. Birbal asked the man to drink wine. The man said, "How can I drink wine in front of the emperor?" But, when Birbal insisted, the man filled the glass with wine and drank it. Soon, he began to feel drowsy. He started pleading

before the emperor, "Lord, please forgive me. I am a very poor man."

Birbal said to the emperor, "This is the quality of a parrot."

After some time, the man drank another glass of wine. In a state of intoxication, he said, "I don't care who you are. You may be the emperor here but I am also the emperor of my house."

"This is the quality of a lion," said Birbal. Birbal again gave the man a glassful of wine. He drank it and fell down on the floor muttering.

Birbal bent down his head and said, "Lord, this is the quality of a donkey."

Thus, Birbal again proved that he was one of the cleverest men of the world. The emperor praised him and gave him many gifts.

THE LESSON IN HOSPITALITY

One day, Birbal went to meet his relatives in another town. But those relatives didn't like any guest. When they saw Birbal coming towards their house, they stood on the dais and pretended to fight among themselves. They thought that when Birbal would see them fighting, he would return back. The man took a long stick in his hand and started shouting. The woman also started shouting loudly.

When Birbal saw the scene, he understood that his relatives do not want him to stay in their house. He thought, 'If I don't teach them a lesson now, they will insult every guest who comes to their house.' Thinking this, Birbal hid

himself behind some sacks which were kept there. For some time, the husband and the wife kept on fighting. The

husband alleged the wife that she had made the dish very spicy. The wife started shouting even more louder. At this, the husband pretended to beat his wife. After some time, they looked for Birbal. When they could not see Birbal, they thought that he had gone. Seeing this, they both started boasting. The wife said, "Look, I was shouting so brilliantly. Birbal could not even think that I was pretending."

"Yes, I also acted so well," said the husband. "I beat you in such a dramatic way that it seemed I am beating you in reality." "Yes, and I was shouting and acting so well that Birbal got afraid and fled away from here," said the wife.

"I didn't flee. I was hiding behind these sacks," said Birbal coming out from behind the sacks. When the husband and wife saw him, they felt very embarrassed. They promised Birbal that they will always give a warm hospitality to their guests.

INVISIBLE TO SUN AND MOON

One day, Emperor Akbar was sitting in his court with his courtiers. They were talking on various topics and were having fun. Suddenly, as usual, a strange question came in the mind of the emperor. He asked, "Can anyone tell me what is the thing

which even the sun and the moon cannot see?" All the courtiers gave answers according to their beliefs. Someone said 'soul', another said 'God' and some other said 'the nether region'. But the emperor did not get satisfied by any answer.

As always had happened, Emperor Akbar looked at Birbal. Birbal stood up and said, "Lord, the thing that even the sun and the moon cannot see is the darkness."

Emperor Akbar liked the answer. He praised Birbal and rewarded him suitably. All the other courtiers felt jealous of the clever and intelligent Birbal.

THOUSAND SHOES

Emperor Akbar and Birbal were very close to each other. They always used to indulge in jokes and funny talks. One day, on being called by the emperor, Birbal reached the palace. He removed his shoes at the door of the royal room and entered it. The emperor quietly asked his attendant to hide the shoes of Birbal. After spending some time, Birbal asked for permission to leave. When he came out, he saw his shoes missing. The emperor also came out and asked Birbal what had happened.

Birbal understood that the emperor was playing a trick on him. He said, "Your Majesty, actually I am searching for my shoes. I had kept them here only but now they are not to be found anywhere. Well, forget it. I will buy a new pair from the market."

"Don't go to the market bare-feet. Let me arrange a new pair of shoes for you," said Akbar. He ordered his attendant to bring a new pair of shoes for Birbal. The attendant in a few minutes came with a new pair of shoes. Birbal wore the shoes and said, "Thanks to you, my lord. May God give you 1000 shoes in heaven." Akbar could not hold his laughter at this.

THE TEST OF THE FAMILY

In the family of Birbal, there lived his wife, his seven year old son and six year old daughter. They were also very intelligent and clever just like Birbal. One day, when Birbal was busy in official work, Akbar decided to test his family members. He put on a disguise and reached Birbal's house. He wanted to ask them a difficult question which they would not be able to answer and proved themselves foolish. Birbal's son and daughter were playing in the corridor of the house. On seeing the emperor in disguise, the son spoke out, "He has come." At this, the daughter said, "But it is not him." On hearing her children, the mother came out. She saw the emperor and said, "Some have and some don't have."

The emperor was surprised to hear all these statements. He couldn't understand them. He had gone to test the family members of Birbal but he

instead fell into the situation of test. The emperor returned to his palace. He changed his clothes and came to his real form. Then, he went to the court and narrated the entire matter to his courtiers. He asked them if anyone could tell the meaning of those statements. The courtiers tried their best but to no avail. Just then, Birbal entered the court after completing his work. The emperor told him the entire story.

Birbal said, "Your Majesty, those remarks were taken from an old story when a stranger had gone to a house when the owner of the house was not present. The first one 'He has come' means that the 'bulls have come'. The second one 'It is not him' means that 'but he has no horns'. The third one 'Some have and some don't have' means that some bulls have horns and some don't have. This means that if one knows that the owner of the house is not present at home, he should not go there. Strangers are still tolerable but if a known person does so, the family members should say these remarks to make him understand his mistake."

The emperor praised Birbal and his family for their intelligence in his heart.

THE FRAUDSTERS

In the city of Agra, there lived an honest moneylender. One day, two frauds came to his shop in disguise of businessmen. One of them said, "Sir, we have some jewellery with us. If you kindly help us in selling it, we will be very grateful to you."

The moneylender said, "Firstly, I will have to get it checked from a jeweller. If it is pure, I can help you in selling it. Do one thing, leave this jewellery with me. I will get it checked by tomorrow. After that, I will try to strike a deal with someone."

The first fraud said at once, "Yes, sure, keep this jewellery with you. But keep one thing in mind. If any one of us comes to take this jewellery, don't give it to him. When we both come together, only then, give us the jewellery." The honest moneylender agreed to what they said. Both the frauds went away. After some time, one of them returned to the moneylender and said, "Please give me the jewellery. We will again come tomorrow with it." When the moneylender asked him about his friend, he said, "He is standing at a distance talking to his friend. He himself has asked me to take the packet of jewellery from you." The moneylender peeped outside the window. He saw the second fraud standing at a distance with another man. He trusted the first man and handed him over the jewellery.

After some time, the second fraud came to the moneylender and asked for the jewellery. The

moneylender was surprised and said, "When you were standing with a man and talking, your friend came to me and took the jewellery." But the fraud  didn't listen to him. He said, "When I told you not to give the jewellery to any one of us, why did you give him the packet? It is clear that you are a cheater. Now, either give me the jewellery or pay its cost."

The moneylender tried a lot to make the fraud understand but to no avail. Many people crowded in front of the shop. Everyone knew that the moneylender was an honest person. They also tried to make the fraud understand but he would not listen to anyone. He said, "I will go to the emperor and complain."

He, then, went to the court and complained to the emperor. The emperor asked Birbal to solve the case. Birbal summoned the moneylender to the court. When the moneylender reached the court, Birbal asked him about the matter. The moneylender told

him the entire matter. Then, Birbal listened to the fraud also. Till now, clever Birbal had understood everything. He said that he would announce his decision the next day.

Both the moneylender and the fraud went to their homes. Birbal asked some of his spies to keep an eye on the fraud. The spies found out his house. They peeped inside the window and saw the two frauds boasting about how they befooled the honest moneylender. They returned to the palace and informed Birbal. Birbal asked the police chief to raid the frauds' house and arrest them. The police arrested the frauds and presented them before Birbal. The two **men** accepted their mistake.

Next day, Birbal told everything in the court. The moneylender was given the jewellery and the frauds were sent to jail. The emperor praised Birbal and gave him many presents.

SELF RESPECT

In the court of Emperor Akbar, there was a courtier named Rehman. He was spending his days in a bad condition as he was repaying the debt of his father to many merchants in the city. Still, he never told this to any of his fellow courtiers or the emperor. He actually didn't want to lose his self respect. He had got only one pair of royal robes to attend the court. After returning from court, he would grind grains in his small mill.

One day, he had lots of grains to grind. He forgot to attend the court. He was engrossed in grinding flour when the emperor passed from there. The cottage of Rehman was in a bad condition. Suddenly, Rehman saw the emperor passing by his cottage. He tried to hide himself but the emperor happened to see him and recognise him.

The emperor wanted to visit Rehman and ask him

about his condition. But as it was not the suitable time, he went ahead.

Rehman didn't go to the court for some days. Emperor Akbar got tense. But, in his busy schedule, he soon forgot about Rehman.

After some days, Rehman came to the court and took his seat. Emperor Akbar entered the court wearing his royal robes in dignified personality. Walking in

between, he reached his royal seat. He sat down and looked at every courtier. His eyes fell on Rehman and he recalled everything. He understood that Rehman would never ask for help because of his self respect. But the emperor wanted to help him. He was thinking of a way to help him without hurting his self respect.

After the dismissal of the court, Emperor Akbar called Birbal and told him the entire matter

Birbal was himself a courtier he knew that Rehman was a man of self respect. He will never ask for help from anyone. He told this fact to the emperor. Akbar said, "I have also understood that he is a man of self respect and will never ask for anyone's help. But I want to help Rehman."

Birbal thought for some time and then told a plan to Akbar. Listening to the plan, the emperor's face glowed with happiness.

Next day, in the court, the emperor signalled to Rehman. Rehman could not understand it and kept his hand on his stomach. Now, there were many corrupt courtiers in the court. When they saw all that, they felt that the emperor had signalled about them to Rehman. At that time, they remained silent. They all waited for the dismissal of the court.

After the court was dismissed, they all went to Rehman and asked him, "Rehman, what was emperor saying to you by making those gestures? What did they mean?"

Rehman said, "Brothers, I really don't know. I myself was unable to understand anything. Therefore, I kept my hand on my stomach. You don't need to worry."

But the courtiers didn't trust Rehman. After trying for much long in vain, they went to Birbal's house. They told him everything and said, "We need your help. Can you tell us what did the emperor signal and what answer did Rehman give?" Birbal was waiting for this moment only.

He said to the courtiers, "This is simple. The emperor was asking Rehman if he knew about the corrupt courtiers of the court. Rehman said that he has got all the secrets in his stomach."

When the corrupt courtiers heard this, they got scared. They went to their houses and brought bags full of gold coins. Then, they all went to

Rehman's house. Giving the bags to Rehman, one of the courtiers said, "Rehman, you are our friend. Why do you want to reveal the secrets to the emperor?

Take these bags and keep your mouth shut." Keeping the bags there, the courtiers went away. After some time, the emperor and Birbal came in disguises. But Rehman recognised them. He made the emperor sit on a chair and kept all the bags at his feet. He said, "Lord, I don't have any right on these bags. Please take these bags." Then Rehman narrated his story and also, how the courtiers had tried to bribe him. The emperor rewarded all the bags to Rehman and returned to his palace.

Next day, the emperor appointed Rehman as a minister and ordered all the corrupt courtiers to resign from their posts. The emperor was very happy with Birbal. Because of him, he was able to help Rehman and identify the corrupt courtiers.

FRIENDSHIP BREAK-UP

A rich merchant lived in the kingdom of Emperor Akbar. His son and Akbar's son were fast friends. They used to spend most of the time together. They had no work to do. They spent the whole day in useless talks. For this reason, their parents were worried about their future.

The emperor and the merchant tried to make their sons understand the reality of life but to no avail. Several attempts were made to break their friendship, but they also proved unsuccessful.

Now, the emperor decided to take the help of Birbal in this matter. He told everything to Birbal. Birbal said, "Your Majesty, don't worry. I will surely break their friendship." The emperor felt relaxed on hearing this.

One day, the merchant's son and Emperor Akbar's son were sitting in a garden. Just then, Birbal reached there and signalled the

emperor's son to come up to him. When the emperor's son went to Birbal, Birbal whispered something in his ears. The prince was surprised. He stared at Birbal and went back to his friend. Birbal also returned to the palace. The prince said to his friend, "I think Birbal has gone mad. He called me and asked me to return to the palace."

The merchant's son couldn't believe it. He thought the prince was lying to him. He mused, 'Birbal is not a fool to call the prince without any reason. He must have said something secret in his ears. But he is not revealing it to me.' But he didn't say anything to the prince.

Two days after, both the friends were again sitting in the same garden. Birbal again went to the garden and did the same thing. Now, the merchant's son was confirmed that something was wrong. He started avoiding the prince. When the prince, saw such a behaviour of the merchant's son, he also became angry. Soon, their friendship broke down and they parted their ways. Both the merchant and the emperor were happy with Birbal. They thanked Birbal and gave him many gifts.

FOUR FOOLS

Emperor Akbar liked to ask strange questions and give strange work's to Birbal. One day, he said to Birbal, "Birbal, I know that there are many fools in my kingdom. But, I want you to present in the court the top four fools of the kingdom." Birbal bowed down and accepted the order.

Birbal started searching for fools in the streets. After a while, he saw a man running away with a plate in his hands. The plate contained a pair  of betel leaf and some sweets. Birbal called out to him, "Listen brother, you seem very happy. What is the matter? Tell me the reason."

But, the man was so much in a hurry that he didn't hear the call of Birbal. Birbal ran after him and stopped him. Then, he disclosed his identity to the man. The man bowed before Birbal. Birbal asked him where he was running to. The man said, "Actually, my wife is getting married to another man. I am going to the ceremony." Birbal was stunned to hear such a foolish talk. He said to him, "You have to accompany me to the emperor." The man got scared on hearing the name of the emperor. He had no option other than to accompany Birbal. After covering some distance, Birbal met a man who was riding a horse. He was himself sitting on the horse but was carrying a bundle of sticks on his head. Birbal was surprised to see this. He stopped the man and asked, "What's the matter? Why don't you keep the bundle on the horseback?"

The man replied, "Sir, my horse is pregnant. She cannot carry so much of weight. She is already carrying me." Birbal asked this man also to accompany him to the emperor. Taking both of them, Birbal reached the court of Emperor Akbar. He said, "Your Majesty, here are the four fools."

The emperor said, "But I could see only two! Where are the other two?"

At this, Birbal said, "Lord, the third fool is you who always asks for such strange things and the fourth fool is me who always fulfills your wishes." Hearing Birbal, Emperor Akbar laughed loudly. Then Birbal told him about the foolishness of the two men. Emperor Akbar laughed more heartily.

THE MILK OF THE BILLY GOAT

Emperor Akbar always wanted to make Birbal speechless. One day, he along with his queen devised an idea to challenge Birbal. They were quite sure that Birbal would not be able to fulfill this challenge. Next day, in the court, Akbar said to Birbal, "Birbal, you think that you are very clever. OK, I challenge you to bring the milk of a billy goat."

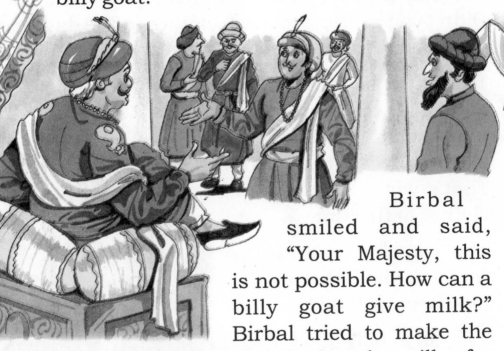

Birbal smiled and said, "Your Majesty, this is not possible. How can a billy goat give milk?" Birbal tried to make the emperor understand that bringing the milk of a billy goat was not possible. Only a nanny goat gave milk, but the emperor was not ready to listen to any excuse. He remained stubborn. At last, Birbal had to accept the challenge. Birbal, then, set off towards his home. He was thinking of an idea to fulfill the challenge. Since he was clever, he soon found out a way. On reaching home, he told the plan to his daughter. The daughter also liked the plan and agreed to act according to it.

That night, Birbal's daughter went to Yamuna river flowing at the backside of the palace. The emperor woke up hearing the noise of washing of clothes. He asked his attendants to present the person who was washing clothes at such an odd hour. The attendants hurried to the banks of the Yamuna and caught Birbal's daughter. Then, they presented her in front of the emperor.

The emperor asked her in anger, "Who are you? Didn't you get time to wash clothes in the daytime? You disturbed me when I was sleeping."

The girl replied, "Sir, actually my father begot a child. I was taking care of him and so, I couldn't wash clothes in the daytime. That's why I was washing clothes at this time."

The emperor spoke out, "Are you mad? How can a man begot a child?"

"Sir, if a billy goat can give milk, then, why can't a man begot a child?"

The emperor was surprised to hear this. "Are you Birbal's daughter?" he asked. "Yes," replied the girl. "My father has sent me here." The emperor understood the whole thing. He gave many gifts to the girl and sent her off.

A SITAR DOESN'T EAT FOOD

One day, Emperor Akbar was strolling with Birbal in the garden. Birbal said that he knew a person who sang very well. He said, "Your Majesty, in my opinion, no one can play sitar better than him in this kingdom." The emperor was a little bit surprised to hear this. After the appointment of Tansen as the royal musician, he had never heard of any other musician. He said to Birbal, "OK, bring him in the palace tomorrow. Invite him for dinner."

Next day, the emperor organised a feast. Many dignitaries and artists were invited. Birbal also reached the palace with the musician. The emperor went to Birbal and asked, "Is this the musician you were talking about?" Birbal nodded his head. Seeing him empty-handed, the emperor asked him, "Where is your sitar?" Why haven't you brought it with you?"

The musician bowed before the emperor and said, "Your majesty, I am here for dinner. My sitar doesn't eat food. That's why I didn't I bring it here." The emperor understood his mistake and kept silent.

GREATER THAN YOU

Once, a drought hit the city of Agra. There was no rain for several weeks. The situation was very tense. Emperor Akbar opened the doors of his water storage for his subjects. He helped the people in all the possible ways. People praised their king for helping them.

One day, Emperor Akbar called Birbal in his private room to discuss about the situation that was prevailing in the kingdom. Both of them sat and talked about the way they could provide help to the far-flung areas.

Suddenly, Birbal felt uneasy. He badly wanted to sneeze. But how could he do that when he was sitting in front of the emperor and discussing an important matter. He tried to resist himself but still couldn't prevent the sneeze.

The emperor said, "Birbal, you are a big fool."

Birbal folded his hands and said, "Your Majesty, I can never be greater than you."

TRADERS BECAME GUARDSMEN

Emperor Akbar was a humorous person. He was very fond of jokes and light conversations. Sometimes, he used to give strange orders in order to test the intelligence of people. Once, the emperor gave order to all the salt and oil traders of his kingdom to guard the city at night. Poor traders! For the entire life, they had only sold salt and oil. How could they guard the city? They all got scared and didn't know what to do. But they had no courage to deny the orders of the emperor. When they could not find a way out of this problem, they decided to go to Birbal and seek his help. They knew that only Birbal could solve their problem.

They all went to Birbal and said, "You have always helped the people at the time of their need. Today we are in a great trouble. We are helpless. Please give us an idea to come out of this problem."

Birbal consoled them and said, "Don't worry. Everything will be all right. Just act according to my plan. Tonight, tie your turbans on your waist and wear the dhotis as turbans on your heads. Every night, the emperor goes for a walk. On seeing you, he will definitely ask you the reason for the strange dress. At that time, tell him everything truthfully."

As Birbal had told them, the traders wore their dhotis as turbans and turbans as dhotis. When the emperor saw them, he got surprised. He asked them about their strange dress. Then the leader of

the traders said with folded hands, "Your Majesty, we are traders. How could we know to dress up like guardsmen? We have spent our whole lives selling oil and salt. We are not aware of the outer world. This is the reason we are dressed like this. We don't know anything about guarding. If we know anything about guarding then why are we traders!"

The emperor understood his mistake. He liked the way the leader told him the truth. He cancelled his order. The traders left for their homes happily.

Emperor Akbar also returned to his palace and laid down on his bed. He thought, 'Such a great idea cannot be of those traders. I think they must have taken the help of someone. Is that someone, Birbal? I must find out." Next day, Emperor Akbar summoned the leader of the traders. The leader got scared. He reached the court and stood in front

of the Emperor with folded hands. The Emperor asked him, "Tell me, who gave you the idea of dressing like that and telling all the things you told me last night."

The leader trembled and said, "Your Majesty, we got scared on hearing your order. Having no other option, we went to Birbal. He gave us the idea. Please forgive us."

Hearing the leader, the emperor stared at Birbal who was smiling. The emperor happily sent-off the leader. Then, he praised Birbal for his intelligence.

THE THREE QUESTIONS

The court was set. Emperor Akbar was busy in his courtly affairs. He was feeling very tired. He thought to kid a little to relax his mind. He asked his courtiers three questions: (1) Whose son is the best? (2) Whose teeth are the best? (3) Which quality is the best?

All the courtiers tried hard to answer the questions. One courtier stood up and said, "Your Majesty, the son of a king is the best, the teeth of an elephant are the best and the best of the qualities is having knowledge." The emperor said nothing and remained quiet. He was not satisfied with the answers. The courtier sat down at his place. Then, another courtier stood up and gave the answers according to his thinking. But the emperor didn't

like his answers also. Like this, many of the courtiers gave answers but the emperor didn't like any one of them.

At last, the emperor looked at Birbal. Birbal stood up at his place and said, "Your Majesty, the son of a cow is the best, the teeth of a plough are the best and the quality of courage is the best." Hearing Birbal, the emperor said to him, "Birbal, prove your answers. Only then I will agree with you."

Birbal said, "The son of a cow is the best because it is used to plough the land. Its dung is used as

manure, which fertilises the land and we all get food. The teeth of a plough are the best because they are used to plough fields which increases the production of food. The best quality is courage. Without it everything is futile. If a person is very able but doesn't have courage, he can't do anything in life."

On hearing Birbal, not only the emperor but all the courtiers got satisfied. Emperor Akbar praised Birbal and gave him lots of presents.

SAINT-COOK-WATER BEARER- DONKEY

One day, in the court, Emperor Akbar asked Birbal, "Birbal, can you solve a riddle?"

"Ask the riddle, Your Majesty," said Birbal. The emperor asked, "Give me the example of a human who is a saint, a cook, a water bearer and a donkey, all at the same time."

Birbal said, "Lord, I will give you the answer of the riddle tomorrow." Birbal went to a house of a brahmin. He put five gold coins in his hands and said, "You only have to come with me to the palace. Leave the rest to me."

Next day, Birbal reached the court with the brahmin. He bowed before the emperor and said, "Your Majesty, this man has all the four qualities which you mentioned yesterday. When he sits down to worship God, he becomes a saint. People love to eat the food made by him. Therefore, he is also a cook. When he goes somewhere, he can be laden with burden of loads. Therefore, he is a donkey. If someone is thirsty, he can act as a water bearer also. In this way, he can perform all the works perfectly." Hearing Birbal, the emperor started laughing loudly. He gave presents to both Birbal and the brahmin.

THE REAL DISGUISE

Emperor Akbar and Birbal often used to roam in the city in disguise so that they could know about the condition of the subjects. One day, when they were wandering in the market place, they saw a large crowd. Emperor Akbar said to Birbal, "Birbal, let's go there and see what the matter is."

Both of them went there and stood amidst the crowd. Actually, a person was showing antics and the people were watching him. Just then, the person beat his drums and said, "Listen, people of Agra city, the greatest disguise has come to your city. Come, if you want to meet him."

As soon as the man said so, a bull came out of a tent and started running here and there. Actually, he was not a bull but a man. But he was acting so wonderfully, that no one was able to recognise him. Some people kept grass in front of him and he ate all the grass. He was imitating just like a bull. Looking at the talent of that disguise, all the people

present there were surprised.

Emperor Akbar himself got impressed by the acting of the man. But there was no reaction on Birbal's face. It seemed that he didn't like the performance of the man. When the man had completed showing his tricks, Birbal picked up a stone and threw it at the disguised bull. As soon as the stone hit him, he shook his body in such a way as if he was a real bull. Now, Birbal also laughed and started clapping. Seeing such a behaviour of Birbal, Emperor Akbar asked him, "When the disguised bull was showing such brilliant antics, you didn't show any reaction and now you are clapping after hitting him with a stone. Why so?"

Birbal laughed and said, "My Lord, an artist can change his disguise quite easily. But only a true artist can copy even the slightest of the emotions. When I hit him with a stone, he shook his body in such a way as if he was a real bull. Then I realised that he is a great artist."

Emperor Akbar got impressed with Birbal. After some time, they returned to the palace.

THE COSTLY CANDLESTICKS

There were many costly candlesticks in the court of Emperor Akbar. The emperor had a great affection for those candlesticks. He had strictly ordered everyone to be careful with those candlesticks. All the servants used to clean them very carefully.

One day, a candlestick was mistakenly broken by a servant. He felt very scared. When the emperor came to know about this, he got furious. He scolded the servant, "Stupid! You don't even know how to clean a candlestick." Next day, the emperor gave the servant the death sentence. For that day, the servant was put into the jail.

When Birbal came to know about it, he felt very upset. He was very sympathetic towards poor people. He went to the jail to meet the servant. He listened to the entire story of the servant. Then, he told him a plan to save himself. Next day, at the time of hanging the servant, his last wish was asked. The

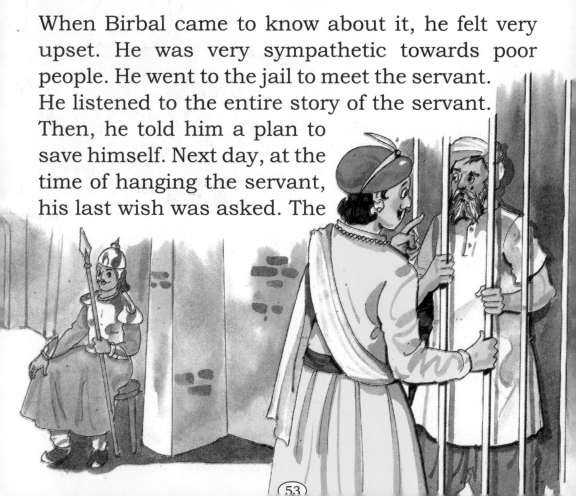

servant wished to meet the emperor for the last time. The soldiers took him to Emperor Akbar for fulfilling his last wish. The emperor was sitting in his room. The servant bowed to the emperor and then suddenly, broke all the candlesticks that were kept there. The emperor, his attendants and his soldiers, were all surprised at this act of the servant.

Emperor Akbar controlling his anger said to the servant, "How dare you break my costly candlesticks in front of me?"

The servant folded his hands and politely said, "Lord, I have just saved the lives of all those people who may get the death sentence because of breaking these candlesticks by mistake. In any case, I have to die, whether I break one candlestick or all of them. Please forgive me."

The emperor was stunned to hear him. He asked him, "Tell me, who gave you this advice?" "Birbal, my lord," replied the servant.

"I am very grateful to Birbal because of whom I got saved from killing an innocent man. I will never get angry at anyone without any reason," said Akbar.

THE ROAD GOT SHORTENED

One day, Emperor Akbar was returning to Agra from Fatehpur Sikri. He was in his palanquin. Some of his soldiers and courtiers were also with him. They were on their horses. The day was very hot and the sun was shining brightly. Emperor Akbar was feeling very hot. Suddenly, he asked his courtiers, "Can't this road be shortened?"

On hearing such a strange question, all the courtiers started staring at each other. Just then, Birbal came nearer to the palanquin and said, "Your Majesty, I can do this but for that you will have to listen to my story." Hearing this, the courtiers and the soldiers thought how could this be possible. How can one shorten the road? Moreover, they were on the shortest route to Agra.

Birbal started narrating an interesting and long story. The story was so nice that everybody got engrossed in it. When the story was about to end, they had reached Agra. The emperor asked Birbal surprisingly, "How did we reach Agra so early?"

"Because I had shortened the road," said Birbal.

LITTLE MORE LITTLE LESS

Birbal's five year old daughter was asking her father for many days to take her to the court. One day, Birbal took her to the court to keep her heart. When the emperor saw the girl, he thought, 'Is she also as intelligent as her

father? Let me test this girl.' He asked the girl, "Dear, do you know Persian?" "Little more little less!" replied the girl.

The emperor could not understand the meaning of the statement. He asked Birbal about it. Birbal said, "She wants to say that she knows little more for the people who don't know Persian and little less for the people who know Persian."

The emperor was surprised to hear this. He understood that the girl was also as intelligent as her father. He gave many gifts to the small girl before she left the palace.

THE REAL THIEF

One day, two men named Hasan and Ahmed came to the court of Emperor Akbar. Hasan was blaming Ahmed that he had stolen his wife's necklace, while Ahmed was saying that he was innocent.

The emperor asked Hasan, "How can you say that Ahmed has stolen the necklace?" Hasan replied, "Lord, I myself saw him running with the necklace in his pocket." Ahmed said, "Your majesty, he is a liar. I am not a thief. He wants to trap me."

Hasan said to the emperor, "OK, ask Ahmed to hold a red hot iron rod in his hands. If he is innocent, God will not burn his hands."

Ahmed was stunned to hear this. He knew that as soon as he would hold the hot iron rod, his hands would get burnt. He had tears in his eyes. He looked at Birbal with some hope.

Till now, Birbal was quietly observing the case. His keen eyes had already understood that Ahmed was innocent and Hasan was trying to trap him. He stood from his seat and said to the emperor, "Your Majesty, I think that Hasan should first hold the red hot iron rod. It will prove that he is truly

seeking justice. If he doesn't get burnt, it will be proved that he is truthful and his complaint is also true."

Hearing Birbal, Hasan was dumbstruck. He knew that soon he would be caught. The emperor had already understood Birbal. He ordered Hasan to hold a hot iron. Now, Hasan started crying. He admitted that he was trying to trap Ahmed. He asked for forgiveness from the emperor. The emperor asked Ahmed to go to his house. Then, he asked his soldiers to put Hasan into the prison. After that, Emperor Akbar praised Birbal for his intelligence.

BIRBAL'S TEST

Most of the courtiers in Emperor Akbar's court were jealous of Birbal. Once, they made a plan to prove themselves more clever than Birbal. One day, a courtier came in the court with a covered pot. He bowed to the king first and then said to Birbal, "Birbal, I want to ask you a question. If you answer this one, we will accept that you are the cleverest in this court else, you have to accept me as cleverer than you." Birbal accepted the challenge. The courtier asked Birbal, "Tell me what is inside this pot?"

Birbal went to the courtier and removed the cloth over the pot. Then he looked inside the pot and said, "There is nothing in the pot. It is empty."

The courtier said, "But you have cheated. You removed the cloth from the pot." "But you didn't keep the condition that I cannot remove the cloth from the pot," said Birbal. The courtier understood that Birbal was certainly cleverer than anyone else in the court.

THE INTELLIGENT ANSWERS

One day, Emperor Akbar was sitting with his courtiers and was kidding with them. Among the courtiers, there was a person who was very jealous of Birbal. He stood up and asked Birbal, "Birbal, answer my three questions. How many stars are there in the sky? Where is the epicentre of the earth? And how many men and women are there in this world?" Birbal laughed and asked an attendant to bring a sheep. When the attendant brought the sheep, Birbal said, "There are as many stars in the sky as hair on this sheep's body. If anyone suspects, he can count the hair." Then, Birbal took everyone to the garden. He fixed a stick in the ground and said, "This is the epicentre of the earth. If anyone suspects, he can measure it."

"The answer to the third question is that there are some people on this earth who cannot be kept in the category of men or women, just like our dear fellow courtier," continued Birbal pointing to the courtier who had asked the questions. The emperor and all the others laughed at the courtier. He went away.

THE FEAR OF THE EMPEROR

One day, Emperor Akbar said to Birbal, "Birbal, my subjects are very obedient towards me. They also love me a lot." Birbal smiled and said, "Lord, I don't think you are right. They really love you but they also fear you. They obey all your orders because they fear you a lot."

The emperor didn't agree with Birbal. Therefore, he decided to find out the truth.

Next day, the emperor made a proclamation that he was going on a hunting expedition, and in his absence everybody would have to pour one glass of milk in a big dish kept outside his palace.

Next day, when the emperor returned from hunting, he learnt that the dish was filled with water instead of milk. The emperor felt disappointed to see this but nothing could be done.

Then Birbal said to him, "Now issue another proclamation that you will yourself check the dish after returning from hunting."

The emperor agreed with Birbal and issued such a proclamation. Next day, Emperor Akbar and Birbal again went on a hunting expedition. On returning back, they checked the dish and found it full of milk up to its brim. Emperor Akbar was shocked. Birbal said to the emperor, "Your Majesty, I was saying to you that your subjects only obey your orders because they fear you. First time, when they didn't know that you will check the dish, they filled it with water. This time when they knew that you were going to check the dish yourself, they filled it with milk."

Emperor Akbar understood the words of Birbal. He thanked him for making him understand the truth.

THE FOOTPRINT OF AN ELEPHANT

Emperor Akbar was tensed for the past few days. The reason was that one of his queens wanted her brother to be made a diwan. Emperor Akbar knew that the man was not fit for the post of diwan. But he was not able to reject the request of the queen. For this reason, he made a way out. He said to his queen, "Listen, first I will test your brother. If he passes the test, I will give him the post." The emperor knew the queen's brother was foolish and would not be able to pass the test.

It was a habit of the emperor that every morning, he used to go to the Yamuna for bathing. That day, he took his brother-in-law also with him. On their way back, the emperor saw the footprint of an elephant. Looking at it, he made a plan to test his brother-in-law. He said to him, "You have to keep an eye on this footprint for three days. If you succeed, I will

appoint you as diwan."

The brother-in-law laughed in his heart and thought, 'This is not a big task. I can do it easily. I was thinking that the great emperor will put me to a difficult test. But he has given me an easy one.' He said to Emperor Akbar, "I will surely pass this test."

Then Emperor Akbar left his brother-in-law there and returned to his palace. The brother-in-law sat there under a tree keeping an eye on the footprint. Without eating or drinking anything, the youth looked after the footprint. Two days passed by. The brother-in-law's condition worsened every moment. But his wish to become the  diwan was compelling him to sit there and look after the footprint. He tried hard to keep a watch on the footprint but on the third day, he fell asleep. Just then, a bull, who was passing by, annihilated the footprint. When the brother-in-law woke up and saw the condition of the footprint, he was shocked. He returned to the palace with a sad face and told the entire story to the emperor. The emperor laughed and said, "I knew that it would happen. Well you go to your sister. She will console you." The brother-in-law went crying to his sister and said, "Sister, the emperor gave me such a work that no one can accomplish." The queen got angry and said, "Don't worry, brother. I will not let injustice being done to you." The queen, then, went to the emperor. She said, "Look, the task you gave to my brother, should also be given to Birbal. If he fails to accomplish the task, you have to appoint my brother as diwan." The emperor had to agree to the queen.

The emperor called Birbal and gave him the same task. He said, "Birbal, if you fail, you will be dethroned from your post." Birbal accepted the challenge and set off towards the banks of the river Yamuna. The emperor had already made a footprint of an elephant there. Birbal saw the

footprint of the elephant and made a plan to look after it for three days. He fixed a thick stick there and tied a hundred yards long rope to it. By then, some of the villagers had gathered there. One villager asked Birbal, "Sir, what are you doing here?"

Birbal said in a commanding voice, "The Royal Majesty has asked me to keep an eye on this footprint for three days. He has also asked me to make all the arrangements for it. To protect this, I think that all the trees and houses in the radius of 200 yards should be demolished. Then only, it can be protected." The villagers got surprised to hear this. The leader said to Birbal, "Sir, why do you want to demolish our houses? We will look after this footprint by turn. No one can harm this mark. Please have trust in us." Birbal agreed to their pleas. He gave the villagers the responsibility to look after the footprint and himself returned to his palace. After three days, Birbal went to the emperor and told him that the footprint was intact in its place. The emperor knew that Birbal could easily accomplish the task. He called his brother-in-law and said, "Look, this is the difference between you and Birbal. You remained hungry and thirsty for three days but still couldn't protect the footprint, whereas Birbal accomplished this task sitting at his home." The brother-in-law understood that he was not worth the post of diwan. He shamefully returned to his home.

TIT FOR TAT

After a long time, the winter season was coming to its end. The weather had become very comfortable. Cool breeze was blowing everywhere. One such morning, Emperor Akbar and Birbal went out for horseback riding on their horses. Like always, Emperor Akbar thought to tease Birbal. He said smilingly, "Asp pidar shum ast."

In Persian language, this statement has two meanings. The first meaning is that this horse belongs to your father and the second meaning is that this horse is your father. Birbal also knew Persian language. He quickly answered, "Daad huzoor ast. This statement also has two meanings. The first being that this is given by you and the second that this is your grandfather. Listening to Birbal's answer, the emperor bent down his face in shame.

IT IS GOD'S GIFT

One day, Emperor Akbar and Birbal were roaming in the streets of Agra, Suddenly, they saw a dog eating a burnt chapati. Just then, Emperor Akbar thought of teasing Birbal. He said to Birbal, "Look Birbal,

this dog is eating filth."

Birbal understood that the emperor was trying to tease him. He said, "But, Your Majesty, this is a God's gift for him."

Emperor Akbar was stunned to hear such an answer from Birbal. He couldn't say anything.

LOOKING FOR SHOES

One day, Emperor Akbar, Birbal and minister Faizi reached a nearby village. They spent the night in a royal guesthouse. In the morning, when they were about to leave, the emperor found his shoes missing. The emperor asked the servants to look for his shoes. The servants started searching for the shoes. Meanwhile, Birbal and Faizi came out of the guesthouse and started waiting for the emperor. After waiting for long, Faizi asked Birbal, "What happened? Why is your majesty taking so long?"

Birbal laughed and said, "He is looking for his shoes." Faizi thought that Birbal was making fun of the emperor. He decided to complain to the emperor about it. Actually, Birbal had hidden the shoes of the emperor. He had hidden them in the luggage of Faizi. After some time, the servants found the shoes in Faizi's luggage. When they told about it to the emperor, he got furious.

Till then, Faizi had entered the guesthouse to complain against Birbal. But the emperor was already angry with Faizi. As soon as he saw him, he shouted at him badly. Faizi could not say even a word. Faizi took a vow never to complain to the emperor about Birbal.

FOOL AND INTELLIGENT

One day, after the court was dismissed, Emperor Akbar asked a question to all his courtiers, "Tell me what is the difference between a fool and an intelligent?"

All the courtiers gave answers according to their thinking. But Emperor Akbar didn't like the answer of any of the courtiers. As usual, he looked at Birbal with hope. Birbal stood up and with folded hands said, "Your Majesty, a person whose mind works quickly at the time of need, is intelligent, whereas a person who cannot respond quickly at difficult times is a foolish person."

Emperor Akbar got impressed with the answer of Birbal. He went up to him and embraced him.

WHAT ELSE? CURRY

Once, Birbal took holidays for some days. He had to go to the marriage of his relative's son. When Birbal was not in the town, Emperor Akbar missed him a lot. After spending his holidays, when Birbal returned to the palace, the emperor was very pleased. He asked Birbal the names of the dishes which he had enjoyed in the marriage ceremony.

Birbal, one by one, made him count the names of the dishes. When he was to utter the name of the last dish, the emperor had to go for an urgent work. After some days, the emperor recalled that Birbal had not told him the name of the last dish. The emperor decided to check the memory of Birbal. He called Birbal and said, "What else?"

Birbal understood that the emperor was asking about the name of the last dish. He said, "What else? Curry." Hearing Birbal's answer, the emperor felt so pleased that he took out his costly necklace and put it around Birbal's neck. When the courtiers saw this, they were surprised. They interpreted that the emperor must be fond of eating curry. For this reason, Birbal got such a costly necklace. They also wanted to receive such costly gifts from the emperor.

Next day, they asked their wives to cook delicious curries. They all filled golden and silver bowls with curries and reached the palace. The bowls were covered with satin clothes. On seeing all this, the emperor was dumbfounded. Before he

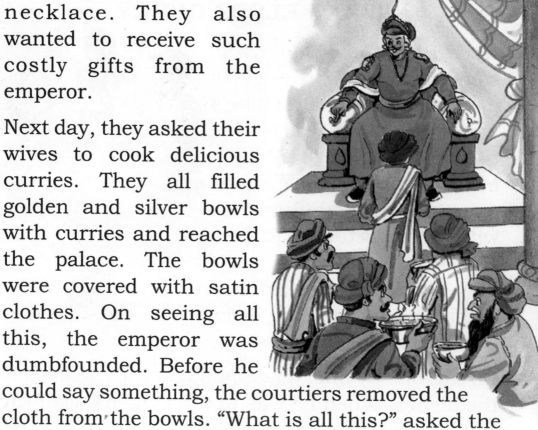

could say something, the courtiers removed the cloth from the bowls. "What is all this?" asked the emperor angrily.

One of the courtiers said, "Your Majesty, yesterday when Birbal uttered the word 'curry', you gave him your costly necklace as a gift. We all thought that you like to eat curry a lot. Therefore, we asked our wives to cook delicious curries for you. I hope you will certainly like them."

On hearing the foolish talks of his courtier, the emperor shouted, "You fools, don't you have any sense. I was asking Birbal what he ate at the marriage party and you people have brought curries for me."

Hearing the emperor, all the courtiers felt bad. They resolved that they will never try to copy anybody without knowing the whole matter.

THE JUSTICE OF GOD

One day, Emperor Akbar asked Birbal, "Birbal, some people in the world are rich, whereas some are poor. Why is it so? If God treats everyone as equal, why has He maintained this difference? It is said that all the people in this world are the children of God. But a father wants good for all his children. He never practices partiality among his children."

Birbal said, "Your Majesty, if God had not done this, the world would not have run smoothly. Think for yourself, you are like a father for all your subjects. But you give one person thousand gold coins as salary and another person five coins. Everyone works for the whole month, why is there so much difference in salary? You cannot run the administration if you don't act like this. You want to do good to all your employees, even then you have to give them unequal salaries."

Birbal again said, "Your Majesty, a person gets the results of his deeds at any cost. This rule applies on the whole world and no one can break it. God never wants that anyone remains hungry and thirsty in this world. But if someone commits mistake, God surely punishes him. When a child commits some mistake then it becomes the duty of his father to scold him  and show him the right path. This doesn't mean that the father doesn't love his child."

The emperor was carefully listening to Birbal. After pausing for some time, Birbal again spoke out, "The riches you see in this world are due to hard work and labour. Those who work hard become rich, and those who are lazy can't achieve anything in life. They become poor and suffer in life."

Emperor Akbar praised Birbal for such a nice explanation.

THE AIR PALACE

Emperor Akbar always gave strange orders to Birbal to test his acumen. Once, he asked Birbal to make a palace in the air. He also kept a condition that no part of the palace should touch the ground.

Birbal very well knew how to deal with such situations. He said to the emperor, "Your Majesty, I need three thousand gold coins and three months to accomplish this task." The emperor asked the treasurer to give Birbal the amount of money he needed and also gave him the desired time. Birbal took that money and went to some bird-trappers and asked them to catch some parrots for him. In a few days, the bird-trappers caught many parrots and gave them to Birbal. Then Birbal gave his daughter, Sushila the responsibility of teaching the parrots. Everyday, Sushila made the parrots repeat some words like – 'bring bricks', 'bring cement', 'make base', 'make a palace', etc. The time passed by. Whenever the emperor asked Birbal about the palace, he would say, "Your Majesty, it is under construction."

When the parrots got expert at saying those phrases, Birbal

said to the emperor, "Your Majesty, please come with me. I want you to see the making of the palace." The emperor was already eager to see the palace. He immediately went with Birbal. Birbal took him to a big ground where all the parrots were kept in cages. When the emperor saw the parrots, he asked Birbal, "What is all this? Why have you kept these parrots in cages?"

"These are not ordinary parrots. They are making a palace in the air for me. I have been training them for last three months," said Birbal.

The emperor wished to see how parrots can make a palace in air. Suddenly, Birbal opened the cages. Parrots started flying in the air. They shouted – 'bring bricks', 'bring cement', 'make base', 'make a palace', etc. "What are these parrots shouting?" asked Akbar.

"Your Majesty, they are collecting materials to build the palace. As soon as they collect them, they will start making the palace," said Birbal.

The emperor started laughing. He knew that Birbal had again defeated him.

THE MANGO TREE

Once, there lived two neighbours named Keshav and Mahesh. One day, a quarrel arose between them because of a mango tree. Each one said that it was his tree. Keshav went to the court and said to Akbar, "Lord, my neighbour Mahesh wants to seize my mango tree. Please do justice."

The emperor summoned Mahesh to the court at once. When Mahesh reached the court, the emperor asked him to tell the truth. Mahesh said, "Lord, actually this tree is mine. I have been taking care of it for the last seven years. Now when the tree has grown and is laden with mangoes, Keshav wants to grab it."

The emperor thought for a long time but couldn't come up with a judgement. He handed over the responsibility of the case to Birbal. Birbal asked Mahesh, "How did you look after the tree?"

Mahesh replied, "Both Keshav and I have appointed a guard to look after the tree." Then the guard was also asked to come to the court. When the guard arrived, Birbal asked him, "For whom do you look after the tree?"

The guard replied, "I work for both of these men. It has only been one month since I am into this job. I cannot tell whose tree is this."

Then Birbal told them that he would decide the case the next day. Next morning, Birbal went to the guard who, at that time, was guarding the tree. Birbal said to him, "You go to the houses of Mahesh and Keshav and tell them that some people are trying to cut the tree forcefully. When you tried to stop them they threatened you. Tell them the exact words. Don't try to be clever. I am sending some of my men after you."

Then Birbal said to two of his trusted servants, "You both go after the guard and see what he tells his masters. Observe the reaction of the two men very carefully. If they are not at home, stay there and wait for them, but I want results."

The two servants

followed the guard. The guard, first, went to Keshav's house. Keshav was not at home. The guard told his wife what Birbal had asked him to. The same happened at Mahesh's house also.

One of the servants stayed back at Keshav's house and the other one at Mahesh's. After some time, Keshav returned to his house. When his wife gave him the news of the mango tree, he smiled and said, "Why should I go there to save the tree? In both the cases, I will be beneficial. Either the tree will get destroyed or I will be declared its owner. Whatever I have done is in my own interest. You don't worry about anything."

On the other side, as soon as Mahesh returned from his work and his wife gave him the news about the mango tree, he set off towards the tree. When his wife tried to stop him, he said, "Please let me go otherwise they will cut down my tree. My hardwork of seven years will go waste."

He took a stick and went towards the tree. Meanwhile, both the servants went to Birbal and told him all the matter. Hearing them, Birbal smiled. He had understood who was the real owner of the tree. Then, Birbal returned to the palace.

When Mahesh reached the tree, he could not see anyone. After waiting for a long time, he returned to his house. Later that day, both Mahesh and Keshav went to the court. Birbal told the entire story of the morning to the courtiers and the emperor.

The emperor said, "The mango tree belongs to Mahesh. Keshav is a liar and a fraud. He tried to harass a simple man and acquire his mango tree. I order Keshav to be put into prison for three years."

When Keshav heard the decision of the emperor, he started crying. He pleaded the emperor to forgive him. Birbal said, "It is important to punish you so that no other man in the kingdom could dare to make false accusations." Then, Birbal asked the soldiers to arrest Keshav and put him behind bars. Mahesh thanked Birbal and the emperor for their true justice and went back home.

LOAN IN THE DREAM

One night, a poor man dreamt that he had taken a loan of hundred gold coins from his friend. In the morning, after waking up, he discussed about it with his family members and neighbours. Slowly, this matter reached the ears of his friend also, who was a cunning man. He decided to take advantage of the situation. He went to the poor man and said, "Last night, you took hundred gold coins from me. Today I am in need of money. Return my hundred gold coins."

Hearing this, the old man laughed and said, "Why are you kidding, my dear friend?"

"I am not kidding," said his friend angrily. "When you take a loan, you owe to return it back."

"What are you saying? How can one take money in dream?" said the poor man.

"I don't know anything. I want my money back. Now tell me, are you giving it back to me or should I go to His Majesty? Then you will have to give my money back and will have to spend some days in jail also. You have told everyone in the village that you owe me hundred gold coins. They will give witness against you," said the clever friend. Now the poor man got frightened. But he had no money. How could he pay hundred gold coins? The clever friend complained against the poor man in the court. As usual, the emperor handed over the case to Birbal.

Birbal summoned the poor man to the court. When the poor man reached the court, Birbal asked both the men to tell everything truly. Birbal listened to their stories carefully. In the end, he understood that the clever friend was trying to befool

the poor man. But, without any proof, he could not be punished. He said to the poor man, "It's OK that you took money in dream but you have to pay it back." Hearing this, the poor man lost his colour, whereas his rogue friend was smiling. Birbal said to the clever friend, "This man is poor. He will not be able to return the loan. Can I give you the hundred gold coins? I hope you don't have any problem."

"No, certainly not. Why would I have any problem? I just want my money back. I don't care who is giving it," said the man. Then, Birbal

ordered his attendants to bring a big mirror. The attendants brought the mirror. Birbal kept the hundred gold coins in front of the mirror in such a way that their reflection could be seen in the mirror. Birbal said to the man, "Do you see the money in the mirror? Take it."

"How is it possible? How can I take that money which is only a reflection?" asked the man. "Why not? If you can give loan in dream, then, why can't you take it back in reflection? Now, are you taking it or I should put you in prison for wasting the time of the court?" said Birbal.

The clever man got scared. He fell down at the feet of Birbal and pleaded him to forgive him. He said, "Please forgive me. I had become greedy. Please don't put me into prison. I am ready to face any other punishment." Birbal felt pity on the man. He asked him to give hundred gold coins as penalty to the poor man. The poor man thanked Birbal for his justice. Both the men, then, went to their homes.

WHOSE FEET ARE BEAUTIFUL

One fine day, Emperor Akbar and his eldest queen were swinging on a ride. Both of them were having much fun. The emperor was wearing his shoes but the queen was barefeet.

Suddenly, while swinging, the queen happened to see her feet. She felt very happy to see her beautiful feet. She said to the emperor, "Listen, look at my feet. Aren't they beautiful?"

Emperor Akbar looked at the feet of the queen and smiled. He thought to tease the queen. He said, "Yes, your feet are really very nice, but my feet are more beautiful." The queen made a face and said strongly that her feet were more beautiful. A quarrel arose among the two. The joke had converted into a quarrel. They started shouting so loudly that some ladies-in-waiting came running there.

The queen asked them, "Tell me truly, whose feet are more beautiful–mine or the emperor's?"

The ladies-in-waiting could not decide what to say. If they answer in favour of the emperor, the queen would get angry and if they answer in favour of the queen, the emperor would become angry.

Just then, Birbal reached

there. He asked the emperor the reason of quarrel. The queen told him the entire matter. Then, she asked Birbal what he thought. Birbal, being clever, said, "Begum Sahiba, I know that your feet are more beautiful but only when your feet are compared with the emperor's feet."

Hearing Birbal's answer, the queen felt pleased. In a way, Birbal praised the feet of both the queen and the emperor. The emperor later praised Birbal for his intelligent and witty answer at the right time.

HEAVEN OR HELL

One day, Birbal went to meet the emperor to discuss about some important matters regarding the kingdom. Birbal came to know that Emperor Akbar was sitting in his royal chamber. He went there and saw the emperor in deep thoughts. He went up to him and shook him a bit.

When the emperor saw Birbal, he shouted, "O you are here. I wanted to talk to you badly. I have some important things to ask you."

At this, Birbal asked, "What is the matter, Your Majesty? What do you want to ask me?"

"Birbal, who goes to heaven after death and who goes to hell?" asked Emperor Akbar.

"Your Majesty, the man who is praised even after his death goes to heaven and the man who is condemned even after his death goes to hell." Emperor Akbar felt happy on getting the answer of his question. He praised Birbal for it.

WHY THE RIVER CRIES

Emperor Akbar had the habit of going for a walk every evening on the banks of river Yamuna. One evening, the emperor was walking on the banks with Birbal. Emperor Akbar heard the noise of the river. He felt as if the river was crying. Emperor Akbar asked Birbal, "Birbal, can you tell why a river cries?"

Birbal laughed and said, "The river leaves his father, the mountain and comes to her husband, the sea. She cries remembering her father." Hearing Birbal, the emperor laughed.

THE ANGER OF EMPEROR AKBAR

One day, Emperor Akbar and Birbal were roaming in the forest when suddenly, Emperor Akbar's eyes fell

on some women who were holding their sarees to make an enclosure. A grunting noise of a woman was coming from inside. Some women were trying to console her. Seeing all this, Emperor Akbar asked Birbal, "Birbal, what is going on there?" Birbal replied, "Lord, the woman who is groaning is pregnant and is going to give birth to a child. The rest of the women are helping her."

The emperor said, "But, they have not made any special arrangements for the delivery. Look, the child is going to take birth without any expenditure. Our queens do not deliver like this. So many celebrations take place at the time of delivery. So many arrangements are made so that the queens do not have to bear any pain. Now I understand that all my queens are extravagant in nature."

Birbal understood that the emperor would not listen to him at any cost. Therefore, he remained silent and went to the palace. After coming back from the forest, Emperor Akbar stopped talking to his queens. All the queens got tensed. They could not think of any reason why the emperor had stopped talking to them. No one dared to ask the emperor the reason. Having no other option, the queens called Birbal and asked him the reason for the anger of the

emperor. Birbal told them the entire story. The eldest queen said to Birbal, "Birbal, you know that there is no fault of ours. Why don't you try to make the emperor understand ? Please do something."

Birbal said, "You very well know the nature of the emperor. He will not understand like this but will get more angry." "Then, what should we do?" asked another queen shedding tears.

"Look, I will tell you a plan. Work according to it," said Birbal and told them the plan.

The queens called all the gardeners and asked them not to look after the garden from that day. What could the gardeners do? They had to obey the orders of the queen. From that day, they stopped giving water and looking after the plants. After a few days, when the emperor saw that all the plants in the garden were dying, he got furious. He called all the gardeners and asked them the reason. One gardener told him, "Lord, what could we do? The queens have asked us not to look after the garden or water the plants. How can we disobey them?"

Emperor Akbar at once went to the queens and asked for an explanation. The eldest queen said, "Dear, if plants in the jungle can grow without any care, then, why can't the plants in our garden?"

The emperor understood what the queens wanted to say. He understood his mistake. He knew who must have given the queens such a brilliant plan. He thanked Birbal from his heart and started living happily with his queens.

THE TRUE TEACHING

One day, Emperor Akbar's spiritual guru, Peer Saheb came to Agra. The emperor himself went out of the city to welcome him and brought him in the palace with respect. Peer Saheb lived in Agra for some days and then, set off for Mecca.

A few days after this, one day, Emperor Akbar asked Birbal, "Birbal, don't you have any spiritual guru to guide you?"

"Yes, I have," said Birbal, "but he doesn't live in any city or town. He lives in the jungle. He doesn't have any relation with this materialistic world. He eats whatever he gets in the jungle. He never accepts any riches and spends his days chanting the name of God. He is now practicing Maunvrat."

Hearing Birbal, Emperor Akbar felt to meet the great saint. He asked Birbal to call his guru to Agra so that he could meet him.

Birbal said, "My guru doesn't go out of the jungle. He only concentrates in God. But since you have asked me to bring him here, I will try my best."

Then Birbal set off for his home. On the way, he met a woodcutter, who after a day's hardwork was returning to his home with a bundle of sticks on his head. The bundle was so heavy that he was unable to walk properly. Birbal went to him and said, "Would you do a work for me? If you

help me, I will give you so much money that you and your family can live your entire life with ease." The woodcutter kept the bundle on the ground and started looking at Birbal with a hope in his eyes. Then Birbal took him to his house. He asked him to freshen up. Birbal then gave him clothes to wear and food to eat. After that, Birbal gave him five bags full of gold coins and said, "You have to do a work for me. For some days, you have to stay in disguise of a saint. Don't worry, you don't have to preach as a saint. Your Majesty and great sardars will come to meet you. But you don't have to fear them. Just keep your mouth shut and sit at one place. They will also give you costly gifts but you'll not touch anything. Keep in mind that in any case, you'll not open your mouth."

The woodcutter nodded his head. Then Birbal applied false beard, moustache and hair to the woodcutter. He also gave him clothes of a saint, a rudraksh necklace and wooden sandals. In a few moments, the woodcutter was looking just like a saint. No one could say whether he was a saint or a woodcutter. For some days, Birbal taught him how to behave like a saint. When the woodcutter became perfect in everything, Birbal decided to take him to the palace. Next morning, Birbal took him to the palace.

Reaching the palace, Birbal made him sit under a tree in the garden and himself went inside the palace to call the emperor. Emperor Akbar was taking his breakfast at that time.

When he saw Birbal, he asked him, "Birbal, did you succeed in bringing your guru?"

"Yes, Your Majesty," said Birbal. "He was not willing to come here but after my pleas, he agreed. But he has one condition, that he will not enter the palace. For this reason, I have made him sit under a tree in the garden."

"What did you say?" exclaimed the emperor. "That great soul is sitting in our garden. We are really blessed that a saint like him has come to our palace. Birbal, quickly send messages to all the sardars about the arrival of the saint, while I am going with my queens to welcome him."

Birbal went to all the sardars and gave them the news. The sardars started arriving at the emperor's palace with costly presents for the saint. By then, the queens were also ready. All of them reached the spot where the woodcutter in the disguise of a saint was sitting. The emperor bowed to the saint and kept costly gifts at his feet. The sardars also followed him. Then, the  emperor said, "You have blessed us by coming here. We didn't even know that a great saint like you lives in our kingdom. Birbal told us about you. Now please have some food."

The woodcutter didn't utter a single word. The emperor again spoke up, "You can ask me for anything. I am the emperor of the whole Hindustan. There is nothing which I cannot give you." Still the saint didn't respond but he was feeling scared thinking that if he continued to keep silent, the emperor might get angry.

Just then, Birbal reached there. Seeing him, the emperor said, "Birbal, your guru is not giving any answer. I know that he is in Maunvrat but atleast he can answer me through gestures."

"No, he can't do it either," said Birbal.

"But why?"asked Emperor Akbar in surprise.

"Because he is scared of you. He doesn't have the courage to speak anything in front of you," said Birbal smilingly.

"What are you saying?" shouted the emperor. "Why will a saint fear saying anything in front of me?"

"Because he is not a saint but a woodcutter," said Birbal and pulled the false beard, hair and moustache. The woodcutter fell at the feet of the emperor and said, "I haven't done anything wrong, My Lord. Birbal asked me to do all this. I was

simply going to the market to sell sticks when Birbal met me. He took me to his house and gave all these costumes and asked me to act like a saint."

"Birbal, is he saying truth?" asked Emperor Akbar strongly.

"Yes, Your Majesty, he is saying the truth," said Birbal bowing down his head. Everyone was shocked at the audacity of Birbal and could not understand why Birbal did all that.

"Why did you do this?" asked Akbar surprisingly.

"Your Majesty," said Birbal, "from past few days I was observing that you were not concentrating on the administrative works and only spending your days amidst gurus, saints, fakirs, etc. Lord, I am not against your practices but you are the emperor of Hindustan. You have many responsibilities and you should fulfill them with full spirit. For this reason, I had to play this drama. I hope that Your Majesty will forgive me for all this."

Emperor Akbar realised his mistake. He said, "Birbal, I am blessed to have a minister like you. You do not need to ask for forgiveness. Infact, I am thankful to you for showing me the right path."

A GHOST STORY

Emperor Akbar often used to find new ways to satirize Birbal. One day, he asked some carpenters to build an almirah, when touched, a person would get stuck to it. The carpenters soon made such

an almirah. Then the emperor put an apple in it.

Next day, when Birbal came to meet him, he asked him to take out the apple from the almirah. The almirah was kept in another room. Poor Birbal didn't know anything about the almirah.

As soon as he put his hands inside to take out the apple, his hands got stuck. He tried a lot to free his hands but all in vain. Then Birbal took the support of his second hand but it also got stuck. Now, Birbal was very tense. There was no one else in the room who could make him free.

On the other hand, when Birbal took a long time to

return, Emperor Akbar felt very happy. He felt that he had succeeded in his plan. He stood up from his throne and tiptoed to the room. Birbal was still stuck with the almirah and was trying his best to free himself. The emperor laughed out loudly at this and said to Birbal, "What happened, Birbal? Have you left your intelligence at home today?"

Birbal had no answer to this question. The emperor understood that Birbal was feeling very embarrassed. Akbar with some men freed him and asked him to return home. But after that, whenever Emperor Akbar met Birbal, he would ask only one question, " Birbal, how was the ghost of the apple?" Hearing this, Birbal would feel ashamed and the emperor felt glad. The emperor had made it a daily routine.

Now Birbal also made a plan to teach the emperor a lesson. He took a month's leave on account of going for a pilgrimage. Birbal left from Agra but didn't go anywhere. He went to a nearby jungle, disguised himself as a saint, returned to Agra and hid himself in his house. The people of Agra thought that Birbal had gone for a pilgrimage.

One day, Emperor Akbar went on a hunting expedition with some of his ministers and soldiers. Birbal was keeping an account of the activities of the emperor. As soon as he came to know about the hunting expedition, he changed his disguise and went to the jungle. In the jungle, the emperor saw a boar and chased it. He was shooting arrows at it. Soon he got separated from his ministers and soldiers.

The emperor tried hard to hunt the boar but couldn't succeed. The boar went inside a bush and escaped. The emperor decided to return but to his amazement his companions were not to be seen. He tried to return to his palace but couldn't find the way.

Wandering here and there, the emperor reached a pond. He was very tired. He sat under a mango tree to take some rest. Suddenly, a ghost jumped from that tree and stood in front of Emperor Akbar. He had long hair, red eyes and sharp, long teeth.

He stamped his feet and moved forward towards the emperor. The emperor trembled in fear. Somehow, he mustered his courage and said to the ghost, "Please leave me! I promise you that I will never come to this forest again in my life."

"Hahaha...I will not leave you," shouted the ghost.

"Save me! Save me!" shouted Emperor Akbar. The ghost was approaching the emperor. The condition of the emperor worsened. His heartbeat increased. He shouted and fell into a swoon.

When he regained his senses, he found himself in his bedroom. His ministers and soldiers had found him and had brought him back to the palace.

When they had found the emperor, he was unconscious and there was nobody around him. The emperor felt very happy on knowing that nobody knew about his encounter with the ghost.

After taking rest for some days, the emperor got well and he again started going to the court. After some days, he got the news that Birbal had returned from the pilgrimage. As soon as he came to know this, he summoned Birbal. He was dying to meet his consultant, his friend and his minister. In a few moments, Birbal reached the court. The emperor stood up from his throne and embraced Birbal. Then he asked him about the pilgrimage. After some conversation, when Birbal was about to go, the emperor asked him again, "Birbal, how was the ghost of the apple?"

"Just like the ghost of the jungle," replied Birbal.

Emperor Akbar could not believe his ears. He wondered how Birbal came to know about the ghost. After that day, he never asked Birbal that question Birbal.

THE MISERLY MERCHANT

In the city of Agra, once, there lived a miserly merchant. He was such a miser that he sometimes didn't even eat food. One day, he invited some poets at his home. One of the poets recited a poem in praise of the merchant. The merchant liked the poem and praised the poet. He said to his accountant, "Give this poet a thousand gold coins as reward."

When the poet heard this, he praised the merchant. The merchant felt very pleased on hearing his praises. Then, the poet went to the accountant and said, "Didn't you hear what your master said? Give me my reward." The accountant said, "Sir, you don't know my master. He only gives false hopes to people but never fulfills them." When the poet heard this, he got very angry and again went to the merchant and said, "Sethji, you told your accountant to give me thousand gold coins as reward but he is not obeying your orders. He is not ready to give me the money and moreover, he is insulting you." The merchant laughed and said, "The accountant is right. You pleased me by reciting a poem and I pleased you by telling you about the reward. Now, go home and write new poems."

Hearing the words of the merchant, the poet felt very sad and left for his home. On the way, he met Birbal. As Birbal himself liked to hear poems, he knew the poet. Seeing him, he asked him, "Where are you coming from? Why you seem so sad? What happened?" The poet replied, "Sir, one miserly merchant befooled me and also insulted me." "What  happened? Tell me everything clearly," said Birbal. The poet narrated the entire story to Birbal. Birbal got very angry at this. He said to the poet, "If you work according to my plan, then, not only we can teach the merchant a lesson but you can also get your reward money." The poet said, "Sir, I don't want the reward, but I want to teach that merchant a lesson. Please tell me your plan." Then, Birbal told him his plan. Hearing the plan, the poet's face glowed with happiness. He was sure that by working on that plan he could take revenge of his insult from the merchant.

After some days, the poet and Birbal reached the merchant's shop in disguise. Standing near the shop, they started talking about money. Hearing them, the merchant got curious. He thought, "Oh, these merchants are so wealthy. Even a lot of money doesn't seem to be anything to them. I should better befriend them. It can be advantageous." Thinking this, he went to them and said, "Oh! Why are you people standing here under the sun? You may fall sick. Come inside my shop." At first, the disguised Birbal and the poet refused but after some time they went inside the merchant's shop. The merchant said to his servant, "Ramu, what are you doing? Go and fetch cold lassi for these sethjis." The servant ran inside and brought cold lassi for them. Then they started talking and enjoying the cold lassi in between. The merchant got impressed by the sweet talks of Birbal. He thought that they were the richest men in the whole city. After talking for some more time, they left from there. Now, they both started visiting the merchant's shop quite often. Soon, they befriended the merchant. One day, the disguised poet invited the merchant to his house for a feast. He had already got a large mansion on rent for that purpose. On the scheduled day, the merchant reached the mansion. Birbal and the poet welcomed the merchant and took him inside. They sat down on luxurious chairs and started talking. Time kept passing but no one came to serve food. Actually, Birbal and the poet had not got meals

prepared. They had come after taking lunch at their homes. On the other side, the merchant was feeling very hungry. He asked, "How much time is left for the meals?"

The poet was waiting for such an opportunity since many days. He said, "We haven't prepared any meal. We only talked about it to please you." The merchant was surprised to hear this and stared at the poet. Birbal and the poet took off their false beards. Then, Birbal scolded the merchant for his deeds. The merchant had nothing to say. He kept standing there with shame. He asked for forgiveness from the poet and gave him his prize money.

In this way, Birbal taught the miserly merchant a lesson and helped the poet to get his prize money. The poet thanked Birbal and returned home.

THE BIRD THIEF

The winter season had ended and the spring season was knocking at the door. The weather was very pleasant. Emperor

Akbar had started administering from the royal garden. He used to sit under a big mango tree with his favourite pillows. Birbal used to sit by his side.

One day, the court proceedings went on till evening. A businessman came before the emperor and bowed to him. He said, "Your Majesty, I am a businessman from Ajmer. I tour the whole Hindustan because of my work. Some days before, when I reached Dhaka, I saw a golden swan that belonged to a businessman. I can bet that a swan like that cannot be found anywhere else. Its feathers were so beautiful. I understood that such a swan should be in the royal garden of Your

Majesty. For this reason, I bought the swan for one thousand gold coins and set off for Agra. I had kept it inside a golden cage. On reaching Agra, I stayed at an inn. I kept the cage inside my room. I thought that I would present you the swan today. But in the morning when I woke up, I was surprised to see the swan missing. I suspect that some servant might have killed the swan and ate it. I request Your Majesty to find out the thief and punish him."

On hearing the entire matter, the emperor ordered his soldiers to go and arrest the servants of the inn. In a few moments, the soldiers came with the servants. The emperor stared at them and asked, "Tell me clearly, who had stolen the golden swan of this businessman?" All the servants said that they had not stolen the swan. At this critical situation, Emperor Akbar looked at Birbal.

Birbal immediately stood up and said, "I really praise the audacity of the thief. First, he stole the golden swan, then he killed it, and ate its flesh. I can clearly see who the thief is because he had not acted cleverly. One of the feathers of the swan is still in his beard."

Now, the thief was one of the servants only. As soon as he heard this statement of Birbal, he thought that a feather might have got stuck in his beard. Unintentionally, his hands went to his beard. Birbal was waiting for this moment only. He slapped the thief and the thief fell down on the ground. Then, Birbal told everyone about him. The thief got scared. He started pleading in front of the emperor. The emperor said, "You have committed two mistakes. First, you stole the swan and then, you lied. You can't be pardoned."

Then the emperor ordered his soldiers to arrest the thief and put him behind bars. After the soldiers took the thief away, Emperor Akbar stood up and praised Birbal. The businessman also thanked the emperor and Birbal. He was upset that he had lost the swan and could not present it to the emperor. But he was also happy as the thief was arrested. The businessman returned to Ajmer.

THE GIFT

One day, Emperor Akbar was sitting in the court with his courtiers. They were discussing about various matters. Just then an old fakir came there.

The fakir bowed before the emperor and gave him some green leaves. Emperor Akbar thought that the fakir was praying for the prosperity of his kingdom. He asked an attendant to give the fakir hundred gold coins. The fakir thanked the emperor and went away from there. The courtiers couldn't understand why the emperor gave hundred gold coins to the fakir. Emperor told them the meaning of the green leaves.

After some time, a Bengali saint came to the court. He also bowed before the king. He gave some rice and ash to the king. The king misinterpreted its meaning. He thought that the saint wanted his kingdom to scatter just like rice and his throne to convert into ash. Thinking this, the emperor got angry. He asked his soldiers to throw the saint out of the palace.

After some time, Birbal reached there. He met some sardars outside the palace who told him about the fakir and the saint. Birbal didn't like the way the emperor behaved with the saint. He went to the court and said to the emperor, "Your Majesty, you misinterpreted the Bengali saint. In Bengal, rice and ash are treated as prasad of Goddess Kali. Giving you those things, the saint wanted your kingdom to progress leaps and bounds. But, you didn't understand him and insulted him by throwing him out of the palace."

Emperor Akbar realised his mistake. He, at once, sent his soldiers in search of the saint. The soldiers found the saint at some distance. They presented him before the emperor. Emperor Akbar asked for forgiveness from the saint and gave him many gold coins as a reward. The saint blessed the emperor and went away. Emperor Akbar thanked Birbal and embraced him.

FULL MOON OR HALF MOON

Once, Birbal had to go to Kabul for some important task. Seeing his dress and hearing his way of talking, the people of Kabul understood that he was from some other country. When the people asked him about his identity, Birbal revealed that he was from Hindustan. The people suspected that he was a spy of Emperor Akbar. They caught him and presented him before the king of Kabul. The King of Kabul asked him,

"Tell me clearly, who are you and from where have you come?"

"I am a traveller. I am fond of travelling to different places. For this reason, I roam from one city to another," replied Birbal. At this, the king said, "If this is the case, then, you must have seen many kings. Have you ever seen a king like me?"

Birbal bowed his head and said politely, "Your

Majesty, you are like the moon of a full moon night. No one can be like you."

Hearing this, the King of Kabul again asked Birbal, "If I am the moon of a full moon night then what about your emperor?"

Birbal replied, "Your Majesty, my emperor is like the half moon."

The King of Kabul felt very pleased. He freed Birbal. At the time of departure, he presented him many costly jewellery and clothes. On reaching Agra, Birbal told everything to his family and relatives. When the enemies of Birbal came to know about this, they told the matter to the emperor. They said, "Your Majesty, do you know that Birbal addressed the King of Kabul as the moon of full moon night and you as the moon of half moon night. He has insulted you. He should be punished."

The emperor understood that they were saying so as they were jealous of Birbal. But, still, he wanted to see the wit of Birbal.

Next day, as Birbal reached the court, the emperor asked him, "Birbal, I heard that you insulted me. I never expected this from you."

"What insult, Your Majesty? How can I dare do so?" said Birbal bowing his head. "In the court of the King of Kabul, didn't you address him as the moon of full moon night and me as the moon of half moon night?" said the emperor pretending to be angry.

"Your Majesty, I only praised you. The full moon can never increase further but the half moon keeps on increasing. The King of Kabul is the full moon, he has reached his prime. He can never prosper any further, but you are like half moon and will continue to prosper in life."

Hearing the explanation of Birbal, the emperor felt pleased. He gave Birbal the necklace of pearls which he was wearing. The jealous courtiers could not say anything.

THE NEW DIWAN

One day, Emperor Akbar was sitting in a serious posture and was thinking. Just then Birbal came there and started kidding with the emperor as usual. The emperor became angry and said to Birbal, "Birbal, you have no sense how to behave. I am dismissing you right now. You need not come to the court from tomorrow."

Hearing this, Birbal returned to his home. He thought, 'I know the emperor himself will call me when his anger calms down.' But he was wrong. The emperor was not thinking this way. He was thinking that Birbal himself would come to the court. When Birbal didn't go to the court for one month, the emperor recruited a new diwan.

When Birbal came to know about this, he became sad. He had no affection for the post, but he wanted to use his post for the betterment of the kingdom and its people. He left Agra and went somewhere else. Nobody knew where he had gone.

Now, the whole burden of the administration was on the shoulders of the new diwan. He was working very hard and trying his best, but Birbal was Birbal. How could anyone compete with him? The emperor was also not satisfied with him. He wanted the most suitable person for this post. For this reason, he made an announcement, 'After a month, a competition would be held in the court. In that competition, one who would answer all the questions of the courtiers, would be chosen as the diwan.' All the willing candidates started preparing for the competition.

Finally, the day of the competition arrived. All the competitors reached the court. That day, only the main courtiers were allowed to enter the court. There were only five contestants for the post of diwan. Among them, one was a man who looked like a poor farmer. He was wearing an old kurta-pyjama and a turban on his head. The courtiers laughed at the man and said, "Look, he has also come to become a diwan. I think he has never seen

himself in the mirror." The emperor had still not arrived in the court.

At the right time, the emperor arrived in the court and ordered the courtiers to start the competition. Abul Fazl stood up and said, "All the contestants would be asked five questions each. One who would not be able to answer even a single question will be thrown out of the contest." Then King Todar Mal asked the first question, "Which is the most dangerous thing in the world?"

One contestant said tiger, other said, lion, somebody said snake or shark. At last, the turn of the farmer came. He said with ease, "The most dangerous thing in the world is death." All the courtiers praised the farmer. They were shocked to hear such an intelligent answer from someone whom they were treating as dumb. So, except that farmer all the contestants moved out from the first round.

Then, Abdul Rahim Khankhana asked, "What gives a person the maximum happiness?"

"Health," was the answer of the farmer. Hearing the answer, all the courtiers clapped.

Faizi asked the third question, "Which is the best weapon?"

"Brain," said the farmer. The emperor was also surprised to hear such intelligent answers from a mere farmer.

King Man Singh asked the fourth question, "If sugar and sand are dissolved in water, how can we separate them?"

The farmer replied, "I will pour the solution into the ground. The ants will eat the sugar and the sand will get separated." The emperor was gladdened. He thought that he will again get a diwan as intelligent as Birbal.

The fifth question was asked by King Bhagwan Das. He asked, "Which other thing burns a person other than tension?"

"Pyre," was the answer of the farmer. The whole court echoed with clapping. Emperor Akbar himself ascended from his throne and patted the shoulders of the farmer. Then, he called

an attendant and said, "Take him and give him a bath. Then, make him dress like a diwan."

Just then the farmer said, "Lord, I don't think I am worth sitting on the seat on which once Birbal used to sit."

"Why do you think that you will not be able to disburse your responsibilities as a diwan? I am giving you this post after taking your test. You are worth it," said the emperor.

"Your Majesty, after being dismissed, if Birbal had come to you to seek forgiveness, would you have forgiven him?" asked the farmer.

"Yes, sure," said the emperor.

Hearing this, the farmer removed his false beard and moustaches. When everyone saw the real face, they got shocked. It was none other than Birbal. The emperor in happiness embraced him. He said, "Birbal, it is impossible to find a person like you."

THE ROYAL NAIL

One day, during a battle, an emperor got his finger injured. He was treated by the best physicians of his kingdom. After much treatment, the wound healed, but the nail didn't grow on that finger. The emperor got tensed. Out of rage, he threw all the physicians in the prison and said, "You will be freed from the prison only when the nail grows on my finger."

After that, he announced that all the physicians of his kingdom will have to treat his finger. And the physician who would not succeed in healing his finger, would be thrown into prison. The physicians of his kingdom got very worried. They left the kingdom and went to other places. Now, the people of that kingdom faced a new problem. Anyone who suffered even from a minor disease could not be treated and died, as there was no physician to provide medical help.

The news spread like wildfire. It reached Agra also. When Emperor Akbar heard about it, he was surprised. Birbal felt very pitiful for the people of that kingdom. He went to Emperor Akbar and said, "Lord, if you permit me can I visit that kingdom? I will certainly make a way to solve the crisis."

Emperor Akbar readily gave him the permission. Then, Birbal disguised himself as a physician, put some herbs in a bag and reached that kingdom. As soon as the emperor came to know that a physician had come to his kingdom, he summoned him. Birbal soon reached the palace. The emperor said to him, "Hakimji, you

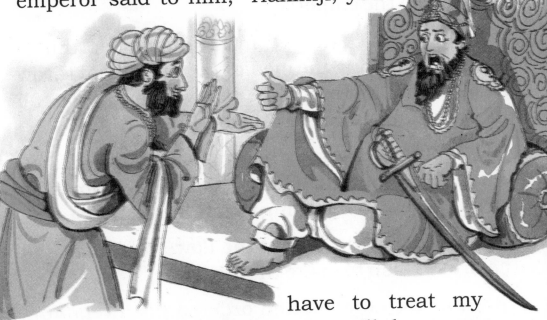

have to treat my finger. If the nail doesn't grow, I will throw you in prison." At this, Birbal said, "Lord, I know the treatment of this disease. I have come here only for this. After taking my medicines, within a week the nail will grow on your finger. If I don't succeed, you can even give me death sentence."

The emperor felt happy. He said, "No other physician ever talked to me with such confidence. I now believe that the nail will grow on my finger."

Birbal said, "But I need certain things to make the medicine. If you could make them available...."

The emperor interrupted, "You just name those things. I can arrange everything." Birbal said, "Please forgive me, lord. But I don't want to be thrown into prison without any fault." "What do you want to say?" asked the emperor.

"If you couldn't succeed in arranging the things needed for making the medicine, you will not throw me in prison. Not only this, you will have to free all the physicians from the prison," Birbal replied.

"OK, I promise," said the emperor and laughed loudly. He thought, 'This physician is a fool. He doesn't know that nothing is impossible for me.'

Then, Birbal said, "I want the flower of Gular and the urine of fish to make the medicine."

The emperor laughed and ordered his attendants to bring the things needed. Everyone tried but no

one could bring the things needed to make the medicine. The emperor had to free the physicians. He also repented for his fault. The physicians thanked and praised Birbal. When Birbal returned to Agra, Emperor Akbar presented him lots of gifts.

WHO'S CLEVERER

In the court of Emperor Akbar there was a courtier named Mulla Rasgulla. Actually he was a fool but thought that he was an intelligent person. One day, he said to the emperor, "Lord, why did you make Birbal the diwan? I am the most able person of this court. You should have made me the diwan of Agra." The emperor felt pity on his foolishness. Then he said to Birbal, "Do you have to say something on this matter?"

"My Lord, do you remember that a few days ago Mulla Naulakha was also wishing to be the diwan? Do one thing, test both of them. One, who is cleverer, make him the diwan of Agra," said Birbal.

The emperor understood that Birbal wanted to have some fun. Mulla Naulakha was a hot tempered person. If he was called there, it would have been very easy to make him fight with Mulla Rasgulla.

Emperor Akbar summoned Mulla Naulakha. When Mulla Naulakha arrived in the court, Birbal stood up from his seat and said, "Mulla Rasgulla thinks that he is cleverer than you."

As soon as Mulla Naulakha heard this, he got angry and stared at Mulla Rasgulla. Mulla Rasgulla also got angry and started stroking his beard.

"What will happen by stroking your beard?" shouted Mulla Naulakha. "You will not become a diwan by such stupid acts."

"Just shut up your mouth, otherwise, I will break all your teeth," shouted Mulla Rasgulla.

Hearing this, Mulla Naulakha pounced on Mulla Rasgulla and a fierce fight started. At the order of the emperor, the soldiers separated them.

Then, the emperor said to both of them, "You both don't even know how to behave in the court. You don't deserve to be a diwan." Saying this, Emperor Akbar dismissed both of them from the court.

BIRBAL'S STORY

Sometimes, Emperor Akbar and Birbal roamed in the kingdom in disguise to know about the well-being of the subjects. One wintry day, while roaming, they saw two men basking around a bonfire in a garden. They went there and sat under a tree. One of the men sitting there said, "Bhaiya, why are you both sitting there? Come and sit by the bonfire. You will feel better." Emperor Akbar and Birbal sat down by their side. But in a few moments, the fire went off because of lack of firewood. Now, everyone started staring at each other. Because of extreme cold, no one was willing to go and get the firewood.

Just then one man said, "Let's do one thing. Each one of us would narrate a strange incident happen with himself. The person who does not believe that incident will have to bring the firewood." Everyone accepted the proposal.

First of all that man himself started narrating the story, "One day I went to the field to rear my cattle. Suddenly, I heard someone shouting thief, thief. I quickly took all my cattle in my blanket and taking them on my shoulders ran towards my village. The thieves ran after me. Because of such a heavy load it was becoming very hard to run. For this reason, I entered into a watermelon. On entering it, I found that there were many people already hiding inside that melon. I lied there and tried to sleep. Just then a goat ate the melon. A cobra swallowed that goat. Then, a crane ate that cobra and started flying high in the sky. The crane flew above a tree under which an army of a king was taking rest. The crane saw the

elephant of the king eating leaves. It had not tasted an elephant for many days. Therefore, the crane pounced on the elephant and flew in the air taking the elephant along. One soldier hit the crane with an arrow and the elephant fell on the ground. The king ordered his soldiers to pick up the crane so that it could be cooked and eaten. When the chef cut open the stomach of the crane, he found the cobra. When the stomach of the cobra was cut open, the goat came out. The chef cut the goat's stomach also from which the melon appeared. When the melon was cut, many people came out. I was also among them. I reached my house and opened my blanket. Then I wandered around and reached here. Now tell me, do you believe my story?"

"Yes, we believe you," said Birbal and all the other people nodded. No one among them wanted to go to fetch firewood.

The storyteller asked in surprise, "Do you believe that a man can hide inside a melon?"

"Why not?" said Birbal. "When a big banyan tree can be in a small seed then this is also possible." "Yes, this is true," the emperor favoured Birbal.

After this, the second man started his story, "I grow mustard seeds. Sometimes, the plants grow so long and get so strong

that I use axe to cut them. One day, a wild elephant chased me. I quickly climbed up a mustard plant. The elephant in rage held the stem of the plant in his trunk and started rocking it. The mustard seeds started falling from the tree. The elephant smashed all the seeds. In a few moments, a river of oil started flowing there. The elephant drowned in the river. I climbed down the tree and made a bag of the skin of elephant. Then I filled the bag with oil."

"We believe you," said the men present.

Now, it was the emperor's turn to tell the story. He said, "Once an elephant chased me. Just then I saw a container. I went inside it. But that elephant also came inside chasing me. I ran inside the container for  six months to save myself from the mad elephant. At last, I succeeded in coming out of the container. The elephant also tried to come out of the container but his tail could not come out of the spout. I continued my journey and today I am here."

"When the elephant was chasing you, you must have got scared?" asked the first two men.

"That means you believe me," said the king in surprise.

"Of course we do," said the two men.

Now it was the turn of Birbal to narrate an incident. Birbal said, "I am the son of a washerman. Once, I was going to the town with

three servants of mine who were carrying clothes. On the way, we lied under a tree to take some rest. On getting an opportunity, a thief stole my clothes. I asked my servants to chase them. My servants chased them but they never returned. Since then I am looking for them. I am happy that today I met them."

"Really?" everybody looked at Birbal.

"Yes, those servants are you three. The clothes you people are wearing are mine," said Birbal. All the people jumped up in shock. The emperor was also shocked to hear that.

"Do you believe me?" asked Birbal. "Yes," said everyone. "Then, immediately return me my clothes and do all the works which you have left at home," said Birbal showing false anger.

"No, we don't believe you," shouted the two men.

"Then go and fetch the firewood," said Birbal.

The two men started fetching firewood. Birbal and Akbar smiled at them.

THE LOAN

Once, there lived a Marwari seth in Agra. One day, a friend of his, named Ramdin took a loan of five thousand rupees from him.

Much time passed but the friend was not returning the loan. Whenever the seth would go for the money, the friend would run away from the back door. His wife would tell the seth that her husband was not at home.

One day, the seth thought, 'I think, Ramdin isn't intending to pay the loan back. He is harassing me. I should better consult Birbal.'

Now Birbal was a good friend of the seth. The seth went to him to seek his help. When he reached Birbal's house, Birbal gave a warm hospitality to him. Both of them talked for hours. Then Birbal asked him about the reason for his arrival. The seth told him about his problem. Birbal thought about the matter for some time. Then he gave an idea to the seth.

The Marwari seth investigated about the daily schedule of Ramdin. He came to know that every morning, he went to a milkman's house to fetch milk.

Next day, the seth hid himself behind a tree which was on the way of Ramdin. When Ramdin passed from there, the seth came out from his hideout and stood before Ramdin. When Ramdin saw the seth in front of him, he was shocked.

"Good morning, Ramdin. So many days have passed since we last met. So, how are you?" asked the seth. "You are right, sethji," said the scared Ramdin.

"Come, let's go for a walk in the nearby garden," said the seth.

How could Ramdin refuse the proposal of the seth? He agreed and both Ramdin and the seth went towards the garden. They had not reached far when a dacoit came in front of them.

The dacoit took out a knife. He pointed it towards

the seth and Ramdin and shouted, "Either give me all you have or I will kill you."

On seeing the dacoit, both the seth and Ramdin got badly scared. Just then, Ramdin thought of an idea. He took out five thousand rupees from his pocket and giving it to the seth said, "Take this, sethji. I took a loan of five thousand rupees from you. I am returning it back. Now our account is clear."

The seth quickly took the money. He took hundred rupees from it and giving it to the dacoit said, "Take this as your reward." "Thank you, sethji," said the dacoit and took the money.

"What are you doing?" shouted Ramdin. "Why are you giving money to this dacoit?"

"He is not a dacoit but my servant, Bhaiyalal who played this part on my saying. Whatever I did was the idea of diwan Birbal. I had no other option left to extract my money from you," said the seth. Ramdin felt very ashamed and went on his way.

WITTY CHAUBEYJI

One day, the emperor said to Birbal, "I have heard that Chaubeys are very famous. If you happen to meet any Chaubey, bring him to the court."

"OK, Your Majesty," said Birbal. Next day, Birbal met one Chaubeyji. He took him to the court and said to the emperor, "Lord, I have brought Chaubeyji to the court." The emperor asked Chaubeyji, "So, Chaubeyji, where will you go from here?" "Maharaj, I will go to Mathura," answered Chaubeyji. "Give my regards to bhabhiji," said Emperor Akbar.

Chaubeyji said quickly, "OK, my lord. But what to tell to your brother-in-law, Vrindavan if I happen to meet him on the way?" The emperor could not give any answer to this witty question and remained silent. He got impressed and gave many gifts to Chaubeyji.

THE ROYAL TAX

Emperor Akbar was engaged in a battle at the Afghanistan border. For this reason, he was in need of lots of money. When he sought advice from his courtiers, Faizi said, "Lord, I think you should cut some percentage off the salary of each of your employees."

The emperor kept silent. He didn't like the idea. Then, King Mansingh said, "According to me, you should stop the works which you do for the benefit of your subjects for a few days."

The emperor said, "No, I can't do this. Many roads and bridges are at the foot of completion. I cannot stop the work right now."

King Todarmal said, "I think we should again get our land measured. May be, we can find out how much income we can raise. We should try to make every land fertile. Then, we can impose tax on it too and raise our income."

"No, much time is needed for that and I need the money as soon as possible," said the emperor. King Todarmal sat back on his seat.

Then, Mulla Dopyaaza stood up from his seat and said, "Your Majesty, the best option to increase the income is to impose new taxes." The emperor liked the idea. He said, "Yes, I can only go for this idea. When the battle is finished, I will cancel these taxes. When our armies are fighting a battle, the subjects should also help them."

If Birbal would have been there at that moment, he would certainly have not liked the idea. He was never in favour of increasing problems of the poor subjects. But he had gone for pilgrimage and Mulla Dopyaaza succeeded in his plan. Actually, he wanted some of his relatives to become tax collecting officers so that he could take bribes and become rich overnight. He had been making plans since long time back but due to the presence of Birbal in the court, he was not able to succeed. Now in the absence of Birbal, he was free to achieve his goal.

The emperor had already accepted the proposal of imposing new taxes on the subjects. He asked Mullaji, "Mullaji, I will impose taxes but there should be some officials to collect them. Now, what to do about it?"

Mulla Dopyaaza was looking for this opportunity only. He said, "It is easy, my lord. I know some people who are willing to work for Your Majesty. We can appoint them as tax officials." The emperor agreed with Mullaji and appointed the people suggested by him as tax officials.

A few days later, Birbal returned from the pilgrimage. When he came to know about the new taxes, he understood that it was the handiwork of Mulla Dopyaaza. He knew it very well that Mullaji was doing all this to earn black money. If he told this to the emperor straightly, he would think that Birbal was backbiting against Mullaji. Therefore, he decided to wait for the right time.

It had been two months since the new taxes were imposed on the subjects, but the treasure of Emperor Akbar was still empty. He hadn't received even half the money he had hoped would be collected. The emperor got tensed due to this matter. Since Birbal had returned, Emperor Akbar decided to consult him regarding the problem. Next day, he ordered his attendants to call Birbal to the palace. As soon as Birbal entered the chamber of the emperor, the emperor said, "Birbal, after imposing new taxes our treasure is still empty. What could be the reason behind it?"

Birbal, at this, said, "Your Majesty, the officials whom you have appointed for the collection of the taxes are corrupt. They and Mulla Dopyaaza are getting all the money and the treasure is still empty. If you want I can even prove it." "But how?" asked the emperor.

"Arrange a feast this evening. I will prove my contention there only," said Birbal.

That evening, Emperor Akbar arranged for a feast. Everyone including Mulla Dopyaaza and his relatives were enjoying the feast. Just then, Birbal

took a big ice cube and gave it to a courtier and asked him to give it to the emperor. The courtier gave the ice cube to the courtier standing next to him and asked him to pass the cube to the emperor. That courtier passed the ice cube to the next courtier. In this way, after passing through many hands, the ice cube reached the emperor. Till then the size of the ice cube had become very small.

"What do you mean by this, Birbal?" asked the emperor.

"Your Majesty, when I gave the ice cube to the first man, its size was very big, but as it passed through so many hands, it has now become a small one. Similarly, the total tax collections are very high but when they reach your treasure, they become a small amount."

The emperor understood what Birbal was trying to say. He dismissed Mulla Dopyaaza and his relatives from his service.

BIRBAL AS MIND READER

One day, Emperor Akbar was sitting in the court with his courtiers. After whole day's work, he was asking strange questions from his courtiers and was entertaining himself.

Suddenly, the emperor asked everyone a strange question, "Who is the cleverest person in our kingdom?"

There were many courtiers who were jealous of Birbal. They felt it was a golden opportunity to teach a lesson to Birbal.

Among the courtiers present in the court, one courtier stood up and said, "Everyone in this kingdom knows that Birbal is the cleverest person of the kingdom." Actually, in his mind, he was thinking to make Birbal fall in a trap.

"How can you say this?" asked the emperor to that courtier.

"I have heard that Birbal knows how to read the minds of the people," said the courtier.

The emperor understood that the courtier was jealous of Birbal and for that reason he was saying so. He thought, 'Let me see how Birbal takes control of this situation.'

"Birbal, can you tell me what is going on in the mind of this courtier?" asked the emperor pointing towards that same courtier.

"Yes, Your Majesty," replied Birbal. "He is thinking that may you live for hundred years."

"Is Birbal telling the truth?" Emperor Akbar asked the courtier.

The courtier had no option left other than to say yes. He said, "Yes, my lord, Birbal is right. I always pray for you to the God."

The emperor thought, 'It is really very difficult to defeat Birbal in talks.'

DISTRIBUTION OF SWEETS

There was a friend of Birbal who lived in Delhi. Once he sent a box of sweets for Birbal through a servant. When the servant was on his way to Birbal's house, he met Mulla Rasgulla. The servant didn't know him. He asked Mullaji the way to Birbal's house. Mullaji at once replied, "From the next turn, turn left. You will see a pink house. That house belongs to Birbal."

The servant thanked Mullaji and went on towards the house of Birbal. Just then Mullaji called him from behind, "Why are you going to Birbal's house?" "A friend of his lives in Delhi. He has sent sweets for him," said the servant and moved ahead.

Mullaji thought, 'It is a good opportunity to have some sweets. When Birbal would be eating them I would reach his house. Then, he would have to give me some sweets. I better take Mulla Dopyaaza also with me.'

Mulla Rasgulla went to Mulla Dopyaaza's house and told him everything. Mulla Dopyaaza agreed immediately and they both reached the house of

Birbal and knocked at the door. Birbal opened the door. When he saw both the Mullas together, he understood everything. Mulla Rasgulla said to Birbal, "Actually we are also the friends of your Delhi friend. We were thinking if we could eat some sweets sent by him."

Birbal took both of them inside and made them sit in the drawing room. Then, he went inside the

kitchen. In a few moments, Birbal came with two plates in his hands. In one of the plate, there were sweets and in the other one, there were two glasses of water. Birbal kept the plate of sweets in front of himself and the two glasses in front of the two mullas. Both the mullas were stunned. Then Birbal said, "The friend living in Delhi is my friend, therefore, I am eating these sweets. Mulla Rasgulla is his second friend, therefore, I gave him lemonade and Mulla Dopyaaza is the third friend, therefore, I gave him plain water." Then, Birbal started eating the sweets. Both the mullas stared at each other.

INCOMPLETE PAINTINGS

One day, a painter came to the court of Emperor Akbar. He said to the emperor, "Your Majesty, I am a painter and have come from a distant country."

Emperor Akbar asked the painter to draw a painting. For a few days, the painter was busy in painting a portrait of a woman. Then he went to Emperor Akbar and asked him to have a look at his masterpiece.

Emperor Akbar, Birbal and some courtiers went to see the painting made by the painter. They all praised the painter for making such a wonderful painting. But Birbal remained quiet. When the emperor asked him the reason, he said, "Lord, look, one part of the face of the woman is missing."

The emperor laughed and said, "Birbal, you'll not understand this. It is a masterpiece. One needs to imagine the other part of the face."

Some days after this, Akbar discussed with his courtiers that he was searching for a painter who could paint pictures for his new palace. Birbal said that he could do the job, as he had practiced this art a lot and had become an expert painter. Akbar gave the job to him.

After one month of hard work, Birbal informed Akbar that he had completed his work. Akbar and all the courtiers went to the palace to see the paintings. They were shocked to see them. In every painting one or the other part of the body was missing.

On being asked for the reason, Birbal said, "Your Majesty, these all are masterpieces. You have to imagine the missing parts of the paintings." Akbar recalled what he had said to Birbal one month ago. He laughed heartily and embraced Birbal.